The Rector
of
Lower Penzle

Denis Applebee

E–mail   jandch.applebee@virgin.net

Cover by Graham Alder

Whilst the historical characters depicted within the story are real, the incidents in which they are involved are purely imaginary.

Life Publications

The Rector of Lower Penzle

Dedication

My thanks go to Jonathan and Tina for digitising the book and to David and Jan for seeing it through to publication.

Contents

The Rector of Lower Penzle

Introduction

Smuggler's Love concludes the trilogy of tales out of the life of the tiny Cornish village of Lower Penzle. In the previous tales life in the village has been punctuated by adventure, first of an attempt to circumvent the unjust taxes of Sir Richard Crendon and then across the Channel, the excitement of escapes from the Bastille in the French Revolution.

Now in the quieter life of the village, love has blossomed where it was least expected, involving the life of the whole village and somehow infecting the most unlikely villagers in its wake. The highly disciplined life at the rectory is thrown into disarray, both by the rising tide of true love and the terror of an accident which threatens the very foundations of the rector's faith in the providential care of the one in whose service he had trusted and gladly ministered to others. Could he now live out what he has so boldly preached?

The Rector of Lower Penzle

Chapter One

Love is a Many Splendoured Thing

Of his call to the ministry of the Church and of his love for such a ministry there could never be a doubt. He was the faithful parish priest of the Anglican Church of St Matthew Lower Penzle on the Cornish coast. His tall figure and athletic stride also told one that he was in love with life, enjoying the raging winds and dashing spray-filled air of a winter's day as much as the Summer's gentle zephyrs, inviting the swimmer into the clear waters of the bay to join his young parishioners who spent so much time making their own amusement in the sea.

What somewhat mystified his parishioners, at least the lady folk, was his love of singleness when there were so many eligible young ladies crossing the steps of the church porch each Sunday. But it seemed he had somehow and for some reason settled it in his own mind that this should be the case and whilst he joined heartily in all the social life of the village was never better as a preacher than when he ministered at a wedding, that state of bliss seemed never to dawn upon his days. He treated each new baby he christened as though it was his own, yet all felt a certain

9

sadness that whilst he blessed others and their families he sat alone in his study, or by his drawing room fireside as winter closed in upon his rectory and he was heard to play a solitary note on his beloved violin.

Mrs Jones his Welsh housekeeper kept her counsel as the village discussed such matters. She knew her charge was happy and as she had watched him in all the adventures of the past, she coveted no replacement for her own ministries in such a household. If this was his choice, then so be it! He was happy, healthy and a strict disciplinarian, holding, no doubt, many secrets confided in him and seldom sharing a word of local gossip of harm to anyone. For a manly conversation, the Rector would stride up the hill beyond the village to discuss theology with Henry Gritton the Methodist miller with whom he shared a great many truths and doctrinal niceties of John Wesley, hoping one day to set eyes on this renegade Anglican with whom he shared so many convictions.

Love had by no means passed John Trevethin by for as he studied the words for love in the Greek language, he recognised the love of family, friends, the opposite sex and God, all found their satisfaction in giving oneself unreservedly to such a relationship. At the moment he found adequate satisfaction in the latter. But then somehow in the alchemy of life one can never predict the unexpected turn of events that changes the wind direction in the sails and requires an adjustment if one is to weather that change and make progress in the voyage. The Rector was half way through his sermon and most did not notice his momentary loss of concentration, but such it was as he saw somewhat hidden before this moment a stranger sitting with relatives some rows back on the far side of the sanctuary.

He completed his final application of the text and left

the pulpit to take his place in the end stall of the choir. He announced his prayers for the needs of his flock and rounded his intercession with his usual sincere prayer for the Sovereign and Government. The choir sang a quiet "Amen" and John raised himself from his knees and announced the final hymn. As usual it was a strident, victorious climax to a meaningful morning service and as the organ played a quite loud recessional piece, John gathered his books and made his way to the church porch. One by one the congregation shook his hand and passed out into the sunshine. Then came the young lady who had quite taken his eye from his notes and his mind from his subject. Wearing a most attractive bonnet and matching attire, she was introduced as niece of none other than Henry Gritton, the Methodist miller. Henry was not with her, nor yet Mrs Gritton, but one of John's usual congregation. Rather lost for comment, John simply asked if she was now residing with her uncle and hoped she would enjoy however long she was to stay in the district. She in turn said so little that he hardly heard what she had said. She with her accompanying folk, moved out into the bright morning and he continued to greet each of his parishioners until all had left. As usual, he thanked the members of the choir, dashed into the vestry to disrobe and made his way up the hill to the rectory.

It was over lunch that Mrs Jones hazarded a question as to who the young lady was who accompanied Mr and Mrs Perry.

"She is a niece of Henry Gritton, the miller," replied the Rector.

"Oh, and how come she has not attended his Methodist meeting over at Crendon Barton?"

"Now that I do not know and wouldn't dare ask. But one

would think her to be of a family not yet influenced by John Wesley and his friends." Mrs Jones said with tongue in cheek, "Well, she certainly took your mind off your sermon, Rector!"

Somewhat confused the Rector said, "Oh, surely my hesitation was not that obvious?"

Mrs Jones continued, "Well maybe others would not have noticed as I did, but I can see why she would attract anyone's attention with that charming bonnet with all its frills framing a veritable cherub!"

Quietly the Rector added, "Hush, hush Mrs Jones, you speak as though we have no beauties among our normal congregation!"

Monday morning dawned bright and breezy which would normally see the Rector setting out on horseback across the cliff tops, calling occasionally on a distant parishioner. But for some reason he made his way on foot through the village and up the hill to Henry Gritton's mill. It was not unusual for him to visit the mill and to encourage a meaningful friendship with the miller, but this morning there were other thoughts in the Rector's head. The young niece of Henry Gritton had captured the attention of the Rector and he was interested to know if she was to stay in residence for a while.

Dust was everywhere and out of the dusty atmosphere an aproned young woman approached the Rector. Surprised by her appearance he proffered her his hand in greeting and she curtseyed in reply, "I hardly expected to find you hard at work alongside your uncle".

"Oh, it's my choice. I have no desire to sit aimlessly by when there is work to be done. But please come into the milling room as Uncle is up aloft, he'll be down directly. We're not milling but cleaning this morning."

"Well you seem to be very much a part of the family here, Miss Gritton. I hope Henry is not working you too hard."

With heavy steps the miller descended to the room. "I think I hear a familiar voice hereabouts. Good morning to you Rector, I'm pleased to see you, though, tis unusual on a Monday morning."
"Well Henry, it is this fair young lady who is the reason for my visit and she needs not to blush at my saying that. I was honoured by her presence in the congregation yesterday morning and have simply come to greet her and ask, if it is not too impertinent on my part, how long she might be with us?" With a smile the miller answered, "tis almost a year since she lost her mother and an invitation has been long standing for her to spend a while here at the mill." "I'm saddened to hear of your loss my dear, but so glad that you have come to grace us all with your presence. If I may add, I take it that you are not of your uncle's persuasion attending church at St Matthew's? "No", she quietly replied, "I am not a follower of the Reverend John Wesley, but I must add that in conversing with Uncle, I could find much to attract me in that man's theology."
"Ho," replied the Rector in surprise, "I see you are a serious thinker then."
"Why, yes Sir, I have read Mistress Wesley's paper. Such a mother as she must be would encourage one to think deeply."At this the miller invited the Rector to join them in some refreshment.
"It will be nothing more than a cup of tea, you understand, Rector!"
"Indeed my good friend, I would expect nothing stronger from a good Methodist, and very welcome it will

be."

Together the three of them crossed out of the dusty mill and were greeted afresh by Mistress Gritton. "Rector, how come you are not riding this morning, for tis usual on a Monday morning to hear of you riding the cliff tops?"

"Oh, you've caught me there Henry, for I have to admit that this niece of yours caused quite a conversation piece between my good housekeeper and myself at the breakfast table and I felt I must investigate further her visit."

"I'm flattered indeed sir," said Alicia, "but sorry to curtail your ride, for it sounds most exhilarating."

"Indeed it is and may I ask if you ride yourself?" queried the Rector.

"Indeed I do Sir, and if I had a horse I might hope to be invited to one day join your good self, if that is not too presumptuous".

"Indeed it is not and nothing would give me greater pleasure than to have your uncle's permission to invite you to join me at some future date. Do you think we can find your niece a ride Henry?"

"As you speak, Rector, I am thinking of that gentle mare that Daniel Perry has. He bought it recently after shoeing it at his forge. I'm sure he would be delighted to lend it to me gladly."

"It is done then!" said the Rector. "We shall arrange a day and I will bring the ride hither to your mill. "But we are forgetting one thing for which I originally came. As yet I have not been introduced and your good niece remains unnamed."

"My apologies Rector, let me present Alicia Mary Gritton, my late brother's only child." With this formal statement the Rector stood and with a bowing of the head announced his departure. There was a quick and brief peel of laughter in the miller's kitchen and all returned to their morning's activity in the dusty mill.

It was a week later that two riders galloped across the cliff tops above Lower Penzle and something more than a Rector and a member of his congregation enjoyed the morning breeze, the delightful Cornish scenery and an occasional shout to each other. When the two horsemen drew in their reins and caught their breath who could deny that there was more than the ride that had caused their enjoyment. Rector John Trevethin was smitten with cupid's arrow with a dart right to the heart. As for Alicia Mary Gritton the shot was fateful and she had much to say, if fewer words to express her ride into the future when she returned to Gritton's mill later that afternoon.

The Rector of Lower Penzle

Chapter Two

A Dilemma of Housekeeping

"I take it Henry Gritton is happy for you to take one of his 'workers' away from her work?" Mrs Jones said this with tongue in cheek, but the Rector answered her as if it were seriously said.

"Oh yes, I think he is more than happy to see her out of the dusty business of the mill. And seeing we are riding, he feels it to be of the utmost propriety that we enjoy each other's company without a chaperone to guard against the gossip at your sister's hostelry!"

"And is it going to be a regular exercise that you are taking with Mistress Alicia Mary Gritton?" asked Mrs Jones.

"It may well be Mrs Jones, for I find Mistress Gritton a most stimulating companion. Her knowledge of the Scriptures and her thoughtfulness in theological matters is quite amazing."

"Well be that as it may, I cannot help but warn you that tongues will wag, and may be rightly so when the Rector of Lower Penzle is riding out with such a fair young lady, and he a confirmed bachelor!" Chuntered Mrs Jones almost to herself.

"Come, come now, Mrs Jones, are you suggesting that there is more than a theological and equine friendship here?"

"Well, far be it from me to advise you, Sir," said Mrs Jones. "But I have noticed that Mistress Alicia is sitting nearer the front of the church than when she first came to stay at the mill. And I notice somewhat more conversation is about her than the sermon after the service!"

"Now that is something you have noticed, but has not come to my attention, but it leads me to a question for which I need a straight and honest answer."

"Rector, have I ever been dishonest with you or given you doubt as to my integrity?"

"No, no, Mrs Jones, but I respect you and your judgement the more as I have no parent with whom to discuss my personal affairs. I'm sure you are wise and shrewd enough to see that the coming of Alicia Mary Gritton into the parish has been more than an addition to our Sunday congregation. I cannot deny that I have found a friendship and companionship such as I have never before even contemplated and that leads me to ask you this question: if I were ever to take to myself a bride, would you be prepared to remain as my housekeeper?" "Oh, Sir you take me by surprise, for though I have seen more in your relationship with Mistress Alicia than horses and theology, I haven't thought of such ramifications. But Sir, surely it would be for the mistress of the house to make such a decision rather than me. I cannot imagine life apart from the routine of the Rectory, but if it was a change which your happiness involved, I wouldn't hesitate in resigning myself to parting from your good self, however grievous it would surely be to me. You have been the most amazing man of God, Sir. We have been through such adventures together in the days of smuggling and if this is to be a challenge of another chapter in the life of Lower Penzle, then I would step into it with pleasure."

"Mrs Jones, Ma'm, you are the most wonderful woman! I cannot imagine life in the rectory without you and the addition of a mistress to the rectory would not in the least hinder your good ministry. Indeed, if such a change were to hear little feet running around your skirts, surely your ministry would the more be appreciated? Now, I've said more than I intended, but you will keep our conversation to yourself and we shall see if the wind of change is blowing in our favour later today."

"Well, Sir, if by that you mean you are to propose to Mistress Alicia, I shall pray that not only may there be a change of wind, but that the sun will shine on you both."

"Thank you dear Mrs Jones, you are a mother that I never knew in my childhood and I shall ever be thankful for your understanding. I have no doubt that any decision made today will involve your good self in the happiest of understanding."

With a lighter step the Rector rode up the hill to the mill, even his horse seemed to sense the urgency of that journey, for it cantered whereas it would normally trot through the village as the Rector greeted his parishioners. But today his was a mission and he tethered his horse at the mill and strode into Henry Gritton's presence as nervously as if he were on reprimand from the Bishop. "Henry, are you there?"

"Oh, I'm sorry, Rector," said Mrs Gritton, "Henry has had to go across to Crendon Barton, but he will be back shortly. Do come in and wait."

"Well, Mrs Gritton, maybe it is well that I can speak to

you first."

"Why of course you may speak, Rector, what is on your mind?"

"Mrs Gritton, you know my life in the parish has been one of simplicity and I trust faithfulness to my calling. And while I have remained single, it has not been because I hold some Roman view of priestly celibacy. I have remained happily single by choice, I suppose because I have never been attracted to anyone whose partnership I felt could add to my life's ministry and personal happiness. I'm sure there have been many young ladies who would make admirable minister's wives but none who have captured my affection in the slightest way. Please forgive my rambling on but I need to unburden my mind to you and let you understand that I have not come to my present position lightly or without prayer and conviction."

Mrs Gritton coughed a little. "And what, may I ask Sir, is that present position for you must realise that I am a happily married woman and when I made my vows I meant every word of them."

"Oh, Ma'm, I think you misunderstand my intention. I am not seeking your hand and am embarrassed to think that you would think such a thing."

"Rector, I know you have no such intention, so be at ease for if you are seeking a hand I would hazard a guess that it would be Mistress Alicia. And haven't we been expecting such a visit as you are making this morning? And because you are here, that young lady is at this moment hiding up in the mill. Fear not, my good friend you and your request have been anticipated these several days. Henry will welcome you without a moment's hesitation. But have you asked the young lady yet?"

"Well," spluttered the Rector, "No because I wished to have

Henry's blessing first."

"Then why don't you make your way up into the milling room, I think you will find a heart that is beating rather fast as she waits your arrival and whatever it is you have prepared to say." With a simple 'Thank You' the Rector left Mrs Gritton and made his way into the mill and an awaiting fair maiden to make one of the most momentous decisions of his life. This confirmed bachelor was about to surrender his freedom and seek the hand of a lifelong companion.

His entry onto the milling room floor was theatrically timed for as he entered the object of his attraction screamed and fled into his arms! "What on earth is the matter?" he demanded.

"A rat!" she shouted. "The biggest rat I've ever seen."
"Calm down my dear, it will be more afraid of you than you of it."

"Oh, I'm so sorry," she struggled to say." I do apologise Rector, I was not aware that it was you at the door. Please forgive me!"

"My dear, there is nothing to forgive and you have come to the right one whatever the reason for this display of female fear. You are right where you should be even if you have ruined all I had to say at this moment."

There was a breathless silence as she relaxed into his embrace and he bent over her to plant a kiss on her forehead. "I came, my dear Alicia, to ask a serious question and how better to ask it than to hold you in my arms?"

"And what, may I ask is your question Rector?"

"Oh I think it hardly necessary to beat about the bush Alicia; it is that you would consider my hand in marriage. I had come to ask your uncle for that permission which normally I would ask of your father. What say you?"

"Well I think you may have the opportunity to ask my uncle now, for I hear his horse coming into the yard. Come now Rector and then I will give you my answer, too."

The miller walked in on the two and with warm smiles greeted first the Rector, then his niece. The Rector had had no chance to voice his request when Mrs Gritton appeared and called her husband and so the four of them stood silently signalling to each other without a word. Then the Rector spoke: "Henry, I have come to ask for the hand of Alicia, but I would not trespass on your guardianship without first asking your good favour."

"My dear Rector, have we not watched your courtship developing over these weeks since first Alicia arrived. Not once would she forsake her devotion to the Anglican Communion to join us in our Methodist meeting. But I put that aside to simply say, we have nothing but joy in our hearts that Alicia coming into our home has brought love into yours. You have our blessing and we may look to a date not too far ahead, I trust, till we can attend upon the rituals and see Alicia installed as mistress of the Rectory. But tell me my friend, what of our dear Mrs Jones? Is she to return to her Welsh village and leave her sister at The White Horses?"

It was a bright winter's afternoon that found the Gritton's at tea in the Rectory. Mrs Jones handed the last cup of tea to Alicia, placing it on the little side table alongside a plate and napkin. Then she stood in front of each guest and handed a plate of finely cut triangles of potted meat sandwiches. Henry Gritton unashamedly inspected the two sides of his sandwich and Mrs Jones proudly stated that this was her specialty of potted meat. Henry Gritton looked at her and said with the same sense of pride, "And this is some good Gritton's flour!" They all laughed and Mrs Jones excused herself and left the company alone.

"Henry, you asked me a day or so ago of Mrs Jones' future service. I have assured her that her presence in a future married household is in no doubt. Alicia would be free of housekeeping to accompany me on my pastoral visits." "And I suppose Alicia would play her part in some future smuggling projects, too!" This was said with a warm chuckle all round and Alicia made bold as to demand at some future date, a full account of this unorthodox behaviour of a man of 'The Cloth!'

The little company had set this day for some definite discussion regarding the wedding arrangements. And Henry asked if the Bishop of Truro were to be called as upon to conduct the ceremony. "No," said the Rector, "While he would indeed be invited and would no doubt wish to be included in the service, Alicia has requested that John Fletcher, Principal of Trevecca College in Wales and Vicar of Madeley. It was he who so influenced Alicia in her spiritual pilgrimage and set her reading Mistress Wesley's writings. It will be an honour to have him here. You will find a kindred spirit Henry and we shall have at least a moment to fellowship with this saint of God. Now Henry, I take it you will lead the lady to join me on the day and Alicia has suggested that little Donald and Lizzy's daughter, Patsy, should be her bridesmaid. I'll choose the music with Edgar Prendergast and the church sidesmen will attend to the shepherding folk to their seats." "Rector, may I request that we sing one of Charles Wesley's new hymns, which would be of great meaning? *Love Divine all loves excelling, Joy of heaven to earth come down...*"

"That sounds like the ideal closing hymn as we rejoice

in a great day, I trust, in all our lives, and I certainly know it will be a greatly enjoyed day for the parish. In fact the Parish Church Council has taken full responsibility for catering at The White Horses, so we look to be all set. Henry, lead us in a word of prayer, will you?"

"But Rector, you are the priest here, I am but a layman."

"Henry the word of God says we are 'all *priests* and *kings* unto our God', so lead us, please!"

Chapter Three

The Smuggler Loses His Freedom

The days awaiting the wedding seemed long and both full and empty, full of details which needed attention of both bride and bridegroom, empty in that they were still apart. But each Monday after breakfast the two would ride out across the cliff tops and find a place out of the wind to tether their horses and sit and discuss the future, and one might add, explain the past. The Rector knew little of Alicia's family background and Alicia was all ears to hear and understand the history of the smuggler and his escapades, both off the shores of Lower Penzle and over the Channel in France.

Both shared their stories and, as they sat musing on the past, enjoyed each other's company in the present. Their being alone without a chaperone placed a somewhat strong test of discipline upon them both, for as they talked they came to a strong attraction and feelings which John Trevethin had never experienced in his thirty and two years, feelings that expressed themselves as his arm stretched across Alicia's shoulders and pulled her closer to him. Alicia showed not the slightest reserve and John felt a great surge of affection as he leaned across her and kissed her smooth face, her hair falling across his mouth as he did so.

Alarmed at what he felt, he drew back and springing to his feet bent down and catching her hand, drew her to his side.

Then bending to kiss her fervently said, "I think we should be making for Mrs Jones' dinner or we will be late and she will want to know what detained us!" "John," Alicia said with quiet whispered voice, "I trust you and that I will do for all our future love together. You must know that what you are feeling, I too, am feeling and long for the day when there will be no further need to leave unexpressed what we feel for each other."

With that perfect expression of mutual affection they mounted their rides and galloped across the cliff-top path with joyful abandon to arrive with ruddy faces and breathless appetites for Mrs Jones' meal of the day.

The long awaited wedding day at last arrived. The whole village was awash with preparations and no effort was spared to show the affection with which the Rector was held. This was his day and all the past adventures rolled into a great tide of warm and well earned support, a wedding which was to be long remembered by all and much treasured by the Rector and his bride.

Of the service, little need be said; the wording from *The Book of Common Prayer* had been heard and responded to by every couple as they stood before the altar of St Matthews'. The sermon was a model of warmth and humour as John Fletcher spoke of the Wedding of Cana in Galilee, of the disciples' attendance as today the worthy Parish Councillors stood alongside their Rector and recalled the many activities they had experienced. There were, however, other men from the past who stood unexpectedly in their midst, Jack Dart, Pierre Latreque alongside the redoubtable Captain Winton Willoughby Williams. The Bishop of Truro gave his blessing to crown the proceedings and bride and groom made their way back down the aisle to be showered by a thousand rose petals as they emerged into the sunlight and awaiting coach which surprisingly had been provided by Sir Richard Crendon. The Rev and Mrs John Trevethin had stepped into a new chapter of both their own history and that of Lower Penzle and the village was there in strength and completeness to endorse it. Perhaps the only sad note was heard in a tiny cry from Patsy, Donald and Lizzy Creedy's little girl who was kept aside by her mother covered from head to toe with chicken pox and not able to attend the bride as her maid.

The White Horses Inn was festooned with bunting and its parlour boasted a feast fit for a king. The landlord's wife and her sister, Mrs Jones, had a table set for the bridal couple, Henry and Mrs Gritton, the Bishop of Truro, John Fletcher and the chairman of the Parish Church Council. As the other guests arrived from the church, toasts were drunk and speeches made. It seemed nothing had been spared to make this a royal wedding occasion.

The noise and merry making was crowned with music from fiddles and pipes and the dancing led by the bells and sticks of the Morris dancing troop from Crendon Bywater. It was late afternoon when after retiring to change their clothes, the couple were led out to the cheers of the crowded forecourt and the horse impatiently prancing of Sir Richard Crendon's coach which awaited them. Cheered, embraced by their nearest, the happy couple left in a flurry of rose petals for Crendon Bywater. Awaiting them at the quay was Captain Storeton and the *Sea Winkle*. As the tide lifted her out from the mud, with her sails unfurled she nosed her way of the harbour and set her course south and then due west for the Scilly Isles. Making her way carefully as night fell, she tied up at St Mary's harbour side where the vicar of the town was awaiting them. Before night enfolded them they relieved themselves of their heavy cloaks and stood for a moment before embracing with laughter in the realisation that they were alone and free to enjoy their affections as they had for so long restrained and disciplined themselves. Few words were exchanged before they retired for their first night of married bliss: Mr and Mrs John Trevethin, John and Alicia. John had considered the surrender of his freedom as a bachelor, Alicia had thought of her rescue from loneliness which she had suffered following the death of first her father and then her mother, but both knew deep inside their personalities they had gained so much more than they might have ever had before. *'For this reason shall a man leave his father and mother and be joined to his wife, and they shall become one flesh.'*

Swimming, walking, boating, riding, a daily round of relaxation and pleasure had eventually to come to an end and two weeks after the *Sea Winkle* landed them at St Mary's harbour, she was there to meet them and carry them back to Cornwall and the duties of John Trevethin's ministry. The weather, however, was not in their favour and Captain Storeton had little choice but to accept the easterly wind which carried them to Penzance from whence they would board the Plymouth bound coach and the Lower Penzle high road into the village and home.

It was not difficult for Alicia to settle into the rectory routine and she and Mrs Jones found no difficulty in working together to produce a harmonious life for all three of them. Visitors came and went; parish council meetings were held and entertained by the new wife of the Rector as she served them tea on their arrival and hot drinks again before they left. Nothing could have been a greater assurance of their attendance than the sight of Alicia's ministrations and feminine influence about the Rectory; the flowers in the study, the drapery at the windows and the rearrangement of furniture. How could the same house look so different?

One of the interesting visitors to the Rectory was Captain Winton Willoughby Williams. His rotund, short figure standing like a robin on the door step awaiting some crumbs amused Alicia almost to the point where she could have disgraced herself with laughter. But she mastered her emotions and invited him into the hallway. Then he asked if the Rector was in and whether he could see him at this moment. This caused Alicia to invite the Captain into the sitting room.

"May I introduce myself madam? Winton Willoughby Williams Captain, retired, Ma'm!"

"Oh, I'm pleased to meet you sir, having seen you in church and I'm sure the Rector has mentioned your name."

"Oh, Ma'm he is too kind!"

"I'll see if the Rector will come and see you right away." With this she left the Captain to wait and hope that Mrs Jones was perhaps baking this morning.

"The Rector begs you to forgive him a moment and wonders if you may spare a moment to have a little refreshment?"

"Oh, Ma'm, that is so kind but I could not put you to any trouble."

"Well, if you would rather not..."

"Oh no I would be delighted, I'm sure." Mrs Jones was already carrying in a tray of tea cups and her newly baked Welsh cakes. Captain Williams pulled from his pocket a large white handkerchief and tucking it into his collar sat up now like a small child about to be given its meal. Mrs Jones smiled at Alicia and again she had difficulty in not chuckling aloud at this performance. She poured the tea and offered the Captain the Welsh cakes and she could not help but say, "Of course you may prefer not to eat at this hour in the morning, Sir?"

"Oh, Ma'm, I would not wish to offend Mrs Jones by refusing one of her specialities." And with this he helped himself to two of the delicacies, readily accepting the small plate offered.

At this point the Rector entered the room and having served him with tea and a plate of Welsh cakes, the ladies left, taking with them the rest of the cakes, noting Captain Williams' eyes follow the Welsh cakes out of the door. "Now, my good Captain, what brings you to the Rectory other than to experience the delights of Mrs Jones' baking?"

"Ha, ha, Rector, you know me too well, but I do come on a serious note this morning hour." He brushed a shower of crumbs onto his plate from his handkerchief. "I noticed on Sunday that you mentioned the retirement of the sexton from his position. I'm sure we would all wish him well and wish to thank him for his loyal service to the church over perhaps many years."

"That is very kind of you Captain Williams, Ben Crundle has been sexton for some five years since his sea going days came to an end. Now his health is very shaky and he feels he has had to seek other's help at times and he must not put off the day of releasing his post any more.

But tell me, Captain Williams why are you concerned so?"

"Well, it is rather a delicate matter Rector and I hesitate to mention the fact that my army pension is perhaps not all one could wish in these days and keeping my room at the White Horses is a little more than I had realised." "Well, between you and me, Captain I would have thought your friendship with a certain widow lady might have blossomed into an alternative resting place for you in your retirement."

"Ho, Sir you touch on a sore point, for my own hopes were along that way, seeing she has been so kind to invite me in to share her making and enjoy her excellent meals. But such are the vagaries of such friendships that nothing has come of my hopes. May I ask Rector, without wishing to be forward; are the remunerations for such a post reasonable? I do not wish to pry into church matters, Sir, but you see my point I'm sure."

"Oh I do, I do my dear Captain. If you would like, I will put your name before the Parish Council at our next meeting where we would no doubt discuss what remuneration would be appropriate to such a person as yourself." With this statement of intent the Captain had to be content, though he was hoping for a figure of some kind to be stated. Thinking it not appropriate to press for such the Captain stood bowed and allowed the Rector to accompany him to the door. He turned to find Alicia chuckling with Mrs Jones at the kitchen doorway.

The Rector of Lower Penzle

Chapter Four

Love Lies Bleeding

Alicia fitted into the routine of Rectory life as a hand fitting a glove and together with Mrs Jones, found it easy to either give her time to the household activities or leave them happily in the other's hands. There was not a moment of conflict nor ever a sense that one needed to assert themselves or insist on a course of action. Meals were shared at dinner time in the evening unless there were guests with business to discuss, breakfast and lunch were taken in the dining room with just the happy couple alone to begin the day or talk of pastoral matters.

Alicia would often hear of a sick parishioner and ride out to some distant farm to visit and it was to such that she set out this day. The farm she was to visit was at the extreme boundary of the parish and so she warned Mrs Jones that she may be a little late for dinner. Mrs Jones suggested they should perhaps delay the hour as the Rector had no evening engagements and such was readily agreed. The Rector's wife was a keen horsewoman and from her earliest days riding, had hated the side saddle expected of the female mount. She had therefore designed for herself a divided skirt which allowed her to sit astride and yet be in every way decent.

She galloped across field, up moorland paths and down farm lanes, her riding habit tight about her and a close fitting bonnet covering her hair and ears. Her mount seemed to enjoy the afternoon breeze and took the hedges and stone walls with ease. Towards the end of her ride she approached the farm gate and rather than dismount she reined in her horse tightly and gripped his sides with her heels. For a brief moment he hesitated then kicked off and they rose together across the top of the bars. But just as his front fetlocks should have cleared the bar of the gate they clipped it and with the gate not being fastened swung out and caught the horse across its belly. He kicked hard down on the ground and thrust Alicia forward over his head and down onto the ground. The horse followed and fell to one side of her kicking his feet wildly as he did so as his front legs were broken by the fall. Alicia fell silently but the horse whinnied as he cried out in pain.

The sound carried across the fields where a ploughman was standing for a moment surveying his work. Alarmed by the cry he stood for just a moment before running across the fields to where the sorry couple lay, the woman still as death, the horse flailing its legs as it attempted to raise itself, all the time endangering further the woman who lay motionless close by him.

Grasping the reins the farm hand attempted to pull the horse away from the woman. As he did so a second hand joined him and shouted back to the farm for further help. A woman ran down the lane towards the gate screaming as she saw the woman curled up on the ground.

"Is she dead?" she asked. "I haven't touched her but she

has taken a pretty fall by the look of it. I'm thinking her neck will be broke! Oh, please God, no! But who is she, poor dear? She was riding cross saddle and that's not usual. Oh, then I know who she be, for 'tis all the talk of Lower Penzle that it be Mistress Trevethin the Rector's wife."

By now several folk had gathered and the farmer quickly summed up the state of the horse.

"I'll get my gun, the poor brute needs putting out of his agony."

He left the woman bending over Alicia and she quickly cried, "Oh, good God, she's still breathing, we must get her to the house. You men take off your shirts and make a cradle to carry her."

As they lifted Alicia her bonnet fell off and revealed blood already congealing in her hair. Carefully they carried her into the farm house and as they did so a shot rang out from the gateway to tell them the horse was out of his pain. But what, they asked each other, should they do for their guest, now stretched upon the large farm kitchen table?

Alicia made not the slightest movement apart from a shallow breathing, discernable only as one bent near her mouth. Her breast hardly lifted in her unconscious state. "John," said the older woman of the household, "take the horse and ride to the Rector, but be careful to say she still lives and we may pray that she will remain with us till he arrives."

Riding like the wind, the Rector passed the dead horse which still lay in the gateway and he cried out in prayer that his beloved might not be in such a condition as her poor ride. He entered the silent kitchen as all stood around, caps in their hands as the Rector bent over his beloved wife and prayed in such an agony that the women cried out with him in their fellow agony. Helpless, they could only stand and share the grief of this terrifying moment.

The Rector straightened up and looked around. "Thank you dear people for your kindness. Could I ask one of the men to ride to the village and seek Master Peirpoint and ask him to find some conveyance to bare Mistress Trevethin home?"

"We will gladly wrap her in blankets, Rector. May we wash her dear head of all that blood?"

"Thank you! You have all been most kind, may God be as kind to my beloved Alicia," said the Rector.

It was a sad moment when villagers who had all heard of this terrible accident gathered near the Rectory to witness the Rector himself carry the body of his wife in through the front door. Mrs Jones had prepared her bed and attended every need as she undressed her mistress, bathed and then sought to comfort the Rector. Later she quietly left her sister who had come up from the White Horses to help watch over the patient while she went into the church down the hill. There she found the Rector kneeling before the altar and quietly weeping with the continual breathing of two words: "Oh, God ... oh, God." Daring to kneel alongside her master, Mrs Jones put her hand on top of the Rector's and in a broken voice said to him, "Sir, there is something you need to know."

"What can this be my dear Mrs Jones? What is there that I did not know that perhaps Alicia should have told me?" "Sir, your wife was going to tell you this evening." "Well, what is it woman? Tell me, tell me!"

"Sir, your wife told me this morning that she believed herself to be with child."

"Oh God, what now? Am I Job that I should lose my child as I lose my wife? Oh God, have mercy upon us."

Slowly the Rector's cry subsided and he raised himself

from his knees and together with his housekeeper, he made his way back to the Rectory. Outside stood the carriage of Sir Richard Crendon. The man himself was awaiting the Rector's return and stood to greet him. He expressed his sorrow and then said in a quiet voice. "I am about to travel to Truro, where I know there is a doctor. I will bid him come directly. He will know how best to treat your dear wife, Sir, you can be sure we will send as far as London if need be. Nothing will prevent us doing all we can to save her life and heal her injuries." "You are too kind Sir Richard, I am grateful for your concern. I fear the worst for my dear one as she shows no sign of movement of any kind."

"Good Sir, have you not often encouraged your parishioners to trust in the good hand of our God? Then let me say that all who hear of this day will be beseeching the Almighty for His mercies."

"Thank you, thank you, indeed I must trust in the One who brought me this treasure to preserve her not only for me, but for all in the parish, for was she not this very day going to visit those who were sick?"

Sir Richard ordered his coach away and the Rector regained his watch. All night he sat, his hand upon the cold brow, listening for the almost silent breathing of his beloved. As dawn filled the room with light there was a stirring of the body upon which his hand had laid all night.

She slowly turned towards him and whispered like a breath of wind, "Darling, where am I?"

"Thank God! Thank God! You are awake. You are here in your own bed, my darling and I, John, am here awaiting your waking. What do you feel? Have you pain anywhere?"

"My head hurts badly, but tell me what happened,

where have I been?"

"Why you have had a fall from your horse and we have carried you home. You will want a drink, dear, what can I get you?" But before John could move Alicia had drifted back into unconsciousness and John settled again with his hand on hers. Soon Mrs Jones tapped softly on the bedroom door and entered to see that John too slept, his head upon the sheets, his knees on the floor at the side of the bed. She was about to leave when John awoke and said, "She has been awake, she spoke just a word or two."

"Oh, Sir that is the best of news. I will make a drink for her in case she awakes again and you, Sir, must have some breakfast. Shall I bring it up to you or will you come down and have it before you rest yourself?"

"I think a cup of tea would be all I need just yet, but later you and I will eat together a little breakfast."

Again, later in the morning the patient awakened and this time Mrs Jones was there to witness the stirring and slight movement of the prostrate body. The head was swollen and whilst it showed little of the wound it must have suffered beneath the hair a terrible bruise was showing. As Alicia stirred, John asked again if there was anything she desired.

"Oh John, may we have a light? It is so dark I cannot see you."

"But my dear..."

Mrs Jones gripped his arm and put her finger to her lips. "Sir, be still, she cannot see!"

"Oh, God!" The Rector looked from the patient to Mrs Jones and mouthed the words he could not speak: "She's blind!"

The two horses stood steaming as the coach drew up outside the Rectory entrance. An elderly and a young man stepped down from its interior and were welcomed into the hall. Mrs Jones asked if they would leave their coats with her and then she led them up the stairs to the bedroom. John Trevethin stood to greet the two men with tears freely running down his cheeks.

"Tell me what you know of her fall and then I will seek to examine your wife, Rector." The Rector told the little he himself had been told of the fateful fall from the horse. He told of the horse being killed after injuring itself as it threw Alicia over its head and collapsed.

"Let me feel her head, Sir, and my assistant will inspect her body for fractures."

Slowly the doctor moved his hands over the skull, feeling for any abnormality and then the neck and shoulders. He invited his assistant to follow the same procedure. The assistant said quietly that he found no fractures in the lower body but felt some clear lines of concern in the head, especially at the front of the cranium.

"Has the patient awakened at all, Sir?"

"Why yes twice for just a few moments and then has returned to sleep or unconsciousness."

"Did she speak at all?"

"Why yes she knew me, but this last time she asked for a light to be brought saying it was very dark, yet it was broad daylight in the room. Doctor, does that mean that she is blind?"

"That would seem to be the case good Sir, but this is but a few hours since the injury was sustained, early days, early days."

"Could this be but a temporary condition then?"

"It is far too early to say and we cannot make any tests until she awakes and can respond to our attention. Is she in normal good health Rector?"

"Why yes in perfect health." Then John remembered what Mrs Jones had told him. "Oh, I understand from my good housekeeper that my wife had confided in her just yesterday morning that she thought she was with child. Could this be the case?"

"Well, good Sir, you are the best one to tell us if you were expecting such news, and if so such anticipation would certainly add a complication to our thinking and expectation. Such a shock to the system could end such a pregnancy, but on the other hand the body is resilient and protective of the womb and its contents. But Sir this is a double concern for you I realise. A fearful fall, blindness and a pregnancy. My dear Sir you must be beside yourself with anxiety and rightly so. Never have you needed your faith more than now."

"Indeed good Sir, indeed! I cast myself on the mercy of God, for with due respect to you, I see little medicine can do for such a case as this. But then I insult you good Sir and that I did not mean to do."

"No, no, good Rector, I understand your sentiments. Let us leave this room a while and talk somewhere else, may we?"

The discussion went on a while as the doctor tried to explain in the kindest terms the prognosis as he saw it. He suggested that it might be a worthwhile measure to apply leeches to the temple in the hope that relieving the blood from behind the eye might clear the vision, but nothing could be promised with any certainty.

"I am in your hands entirely, Doctor, and whatever you feel we can try, I am willing. We can only hope that she will awake and satisfy your hopes that there is no further injury."

"I will remain for a day or two, Rector. Perhaps there is

a tavern in Lower Penzle where my assistant and I could lodge?"

"We would gladly accommodate you here, Sir. But maybe you would rather be away from the patient for awhile. I will send to the White Horses immediately." This done, the doctor and his assistant left them with the understanding that they be sent for as soon as there was sign of consciousness.

The Rector of Lower Penzle

Chapter Five

A Trial of Faith

Henry Gritton stood carefully watching the sack fill with flour. He was alone and he surveyed the heaps of grain which overflowed the byre-like stalls where it had been emptied by the farmer who awaited its delivery, transformed into grey flour, the product of his hard work over a season. There could be no stopping for a few days now. He owed it to the farmers to deliver as promised whatever the cost to energy and health, the work must go on.

He slowly became aware that a boy stood trying to attract his attention above the noise of the grinding mill stones. He came over and bent his ear to hear what the boy was trying to say.

"Mistress Trevethin ... an accident... when? Where?"

The boy stuttered and stammered, till Henry drew him away where he could hear better. When he realised the seriousness of the news, he looked at his work, held his hand to his head and said aloud, "How am I to get away just now?"

But almost as he said the words the great mill stones

43

slowed and literally ground to a halt. Henry looked out of the window and realised that the great sails had stopped. The wind had died. The wind which hardly ever died on his hill top site had died in a moment and he raised the stones by pulling the lever hard down. He ran down to Mrs Gritton with the news he had heard and looked back at the great sails amazed that they were as still as could be. Not a breath of wind. How could this be? Here he was with such devastating news, aware that he could not leave his work, yet now there was no possibility of that work continuing. Was this a miracle of God's mercy, that he could now make his way to his beloved niece's side?

Speedily, Mrs Gritton donned her bonnet and together she and Henry trundled their wagon out of its barn and galloped down the hill to the village, up the church lane and were outside the Rectory it seemed but minutes later.

"Henry, my dear man and Mrs Gritton, you have heard. Thank you for coming. Thank you indeed. We sent word to you last evening, but were told no one was at home." "That is true Rector, for this was our prayer meeting night and we were over at Crendon Barton. But tell me, how is she? What happened? Is she able to speak?" "Henry, Alicia awakes just for a moment but even then she knows little of what is around her, for she has lost her sight!"

"Mercy on us, Rector. You mean she is blind?"

"Yes indeed she is, but I should wait a while before we go up to her as the leeches are still at work on her temples, hoping that some miracle of sight might be restored."

"Me thinks it will need more than a few leeches to clear her sight, Rector, but we will pray as never before that God might have mercy on her and your dear self."

Henry stretched out his arm and placing his hands on the Rector's shoulders, he prayed there and then, and the

Rector said an amen worthy of any Methodist.

"But we have other news to tell you Henry, Alicia was aware that she was with child before this happened, so we have double the need to lay hold on the mercy of God."

"Indeed we have Rector and you may be sure our folk will be fasting and praying during these days of waiting. Now let me tell you of a miracle that has already happened, if you will believe it. I was milling when this news came and determined that nothing would hinder my efforts to complete the grain that was overflowing my store. How would I be able to leave and attend to anything else for days to come? Then your news came by that dear young lad who could hardly tell me for sorrowing. Then, like a miracle the wind died and of course it mattered not how much I wished to continue milling there was no wind and all my efforts were in vain. Then I was free to come this way. Is that not a miracle and augers well for God's over-ruling in this dreadful affair?"

The Rector could but agree and together they stood and surveyed the young body lying prostrate and motionless on the bed. Tears were in their eyes as they noted the extensive bruising which continued to show beneath the locks. The leeches worked away and they retired to leave Mistress Gritton and Mrs Jones to keep watch as the two men left the room.

The doctors left later in the week, but they were to come again several times in the months that followed. The pregnancy developed and all seemed well in that regard, but still Alicia cried again and again for a light as she felt above her to touch the face of whoever spoke. Often John would hold her head between his hands and kiss her and whisper words of comfort and faith. At last she found strength to leave her bed and shakily at first but then with more confident steps she would walk the room, descend the stairs and sit with them at the fireside. The babe in her womb was developing fast and every sign was of a healthy child and not a small babe either. Henry Gritton, her uncle, would pay many a visit in the evenings. Together with John they three of them would converse on theological matters to both John and Henry's delight. Alicia seemed to be accepting her condition of blindness as the days lengthened and her time for delivery drew near. The doctor who had first attended her after the accident had made John promise to call him when they were aware of its imminence and that day dawned when Alicia felt the first pains of labour. A rider was dispatched to Truro and before nightfall the doctor and his assistant were in attendance at the Rectory and all was ready in the room as lamps were lit and not a small company stood at a respectful distance hoping to be the first to hear of this long awaited and somewhat feared child came into the world. How would Alicia manage motherhood to a child she could not see and how would a child respond to such a strange and sad situation?

At first it seemed that the call for the doctor had been premature, but then contractions shortened and the doctors guided the Rector from the room to await until the event was completed and he could see his first born and rejoice with his beloved wife in what he could describe and she could hold close. Alicia was, as always well controlled, but accepting that pain could overcome her usual fortitude and the delivery developed. The doctor gave her his instructions and as she responded and the birth pains increased her cries of pain greatly disturbed the Rector. He dropped onto his knees outside the bedroom door and quietly beseeched the Lord's grace for his wife. But as her distress grew worse he left the landing and made his way down to his study. It was from there that he heard her final scream and he raced back up the stairs. The doctor's assistant stood at the door and prevented his entrance.

Then to his ears came a faint cry of a baby and he heard Mrs Jones, who had been assisting the doctor say aloud to Alicia, "You have a beautiful baby son my dear!" "Thank God, thank God," breathed the Rector and tried to push aside the young doctor.

Then the doctor himself came out of the room and took the Rector by the shoulders. "You may well thank God, Sir, for with the birth has come sight. Your wife can see as well as you or I. Come, greet your wife and I will leave you for a moment as you both thank God for His mercy. You have a fine baby son and a wife who can see him!"

Mrs Jones left the room in tears and closed the door upon the wonderful scene as the Rector, on his knees leaned over the pillows to kiss his wife and place his hands upon the newborn son.

"And his name shall be John Henry," said Alicia as she gently pushed aside her husband's eager kisses.

And in no more than two weeks his father held John Henry above the font as a crowded congregation gathered for the Christening as Alicia stood with tears washing her sight given eyes. Not an eye in the church was dry that day and as the choir sang *Jesu', joy of man's desiring,* John Trevethin wept unashamedly upon the tiny form he held in his arms.

Henry Gritton stood to accept the challenge of God-Father joined by John Trenbeath, chairman of the Parish Council. There were also in that congregation, over-seas strangers who would not consider being absent from such an occasion. Had they not shared great moments in the

Rector's life, how could they not be present when there was so much to give thanks for in the smuggler's life? Following the Christening the Rector and his wife left for Crendon Bywater where Captain Storeton awaited them and later that afternoon the *Sea Winkle* nosed her way out of the harbour and made due west for the Isles of Scilly. There, mother and baby rested for a week in St Mary's and then visited Tresco and St Martin's and enjoyed, as it were, a second honeymoon. Perhaps the greatest joy of all, along with their new baby, was the miracle of sight. The doctor had offered but a suggestion of how in that final moment of the birth the eyes had suddenly cleared and Alicia had screamed as much with joyful surprise as with birth pains.

After two weeks of blissful rest and companionship John Trevethin, Alicia and John Henry took sail again and returned to parish life at Lower Penzle. There to meet them was Mrs Jones. Warm fires burned in the rooms as autumn turned into winter and the parish prepared itself for all the Christmas activities. Amongst those who revelled in his work was Captain Winton Willoughby Williams in his new position as sexton. Sunday for him was a veritable parade as he headed the procession from the vestry up into the choir, his long black gown flowing behind him as in somewhat military precision, he shepherded his charges to their rightful position in the chancel, his staff carried as though it were his badge of authority until it was lodged at his side in the vergers stall. His bow before the altar would have graced St Peter's in Rome much to the amusement of many a low churchman in the congregation.

What he did not enjoy was the task of digging a grave and this especially when the ground was hard with ice or worse when on the rare occasion of snow he had first to find the plot and then labour to have all ready for Jonathan

Peirpoint. Matthew Lomas had retired and the task had been added to that of sexton, much to the chagrin of the good Captain. How he wished for his sergeant Egbert Sigrose to be still his assistant but how he also hoped the man would never see his officer in such a humble task. Bell ringing however was his delight and he did it with aplomb, recalling with some embarrassment the night he set the bells ringing when he was keeping watch for the smugglers. Of this he did not wish to be reminded. But he felt as though such memories were truly a part of his life in Lower Penzle and he went about his present tasks with determination to be his military best. Life in Lower Penzle was back to normal and with the village Captain Williams was well satisfied to be accepted, not least by the good ladies who somehow seemed to be lacking whenever he found an excuse to call upon them.

The Rector of Lower Penzle

Chapter Six

In The Midst of Life...Death

Into the small yard of The White Horses came a small private coach and from the vehicle stepped a lady of some worth. At least her dress and demeanour gave a very strong impression of fashion and wealth as she dismissed the coachman and allowed the servant of the inn to carry her small trunk into the hostelry. Jeremiah Solent, the innkeeper, hurried out to make the newcomer welcome and to invite her into the inn's parlour.

"Good day Madam, welcome to The White Horses!"

"And why exactly should there be several horses mentioned in your inn's name?"

"Oh, Madam, our name is not of literal horses, but rather the white tops to the waves."

"How peculiar, how very peculiar, but no doubt you may have a room suitable for me and if possible a sitting room along with a bedroom suitable for a brief stay hereabouts?"

"Indeed we have Madam and I am sure we can arrange for such a sitting room for you adjoining your bedchamber."

"Thank you innkeeper!"

With this brief introduction the lady was led up to her bedroom and the maids busily engaged in clearing a bed from a front room and carrying in a wing chair suitable for the lady.

"Will you be requiring lunch, Madam?" asked Mrs Solent as she curtseyed to her new customer. "No doubt you would like to refresh yourself and then come down into the rear parlour and we shall have a repast prepared for you."

Lots of whispering among the maids noted the newcomer's fine show of jewellery and clothes.

As lunch was served Captain Williams arrived down stairs and took his usual corner seat in the rear parlour of The White Horses with much coughing and clearing of the throat as he noted the new arrival.

"Madam, may I make bold to welcome you to our community? Winton Willoughby Williams, Captain retired, at your service Ma'm!"

"Oh, I'm pleased to make your acquaintance Sir, I'm sure. Just how you can be of service, I am not sure, but no doubt an opportunity will arise!"

This she said with a superior air which quite took the Captain by surprise. He felt a little demeaned and looked down upon the table before him awaiting his meal in a sense of some humiliation. Who was this newcomer, he thought? How could he regain his sense of dignity an officer of the crown, retired, deserved?

A great fuss was made of the lady as plates were laid and tableware set before her in a way the Captain felt quite suitable for royalty, whereas his own humble place was more or less left to him to arrange as he would. However, he would not complain, as the dear woman had no idea of his position in the community, sexton of the parish and retired captain of an esteemed regiment.

The innkeeper's good wife relayed news of the new comer to his sister, the Rector's housekeeper, when next they met and questions were asked as to the identity of the well dressed and expensively bejewelled lady occupying a veritable suite of two rooms at the inn. No one had ever requested such before and nothing was known of where she had come from or how long she intended to stay. The good lady kept herself very much to herself, venturing into the village to walk to what small shops Lower Penzle had to offer. In the draper's she ventured to inspect the materials in stock and asked if millinery was attempted in the village? In Timothy Wiseman's grocery store she enquired requiring the selection of teas which might be available. She sought to sample both butter and cheese, as though she would be setting up a household, yet actually purchased nothing. The village was a stir with suggestions as to who she was and what she was doing residing a while in such a place as Lower Penzle. In church on Sunday morning she caused a stir as she selected a pew under the supervision of Captain Williams and made quite a fuss of requesting a better Prayer Book than the one first offered her. She paraded from the church to the inn as though she was indeed royalty and acknowledged every nod of the head of the older folk and curtsey of the young ladies. Who was she?

She had given her name to Jeremiah Solent as Mrs Henrietta Benowith, cousin to the Earl of Wentworth. She stated that her residence was in Greenwich, South of London and adjacent to the Royal Observatory. It all sounded very grand, but gave not a hint as to why she should be staying here. As always when news was scarce, rumour thrived and every kind of suggestion was made as to her reasons for being resident with them here in Lower Penzle. Her movements were so limited and her visitors quite non-existent so when a messenger arrived requesting her whereabouts conjecture ran riot. Yet still no genuine understanding came. The Rector paid a courteous visit some weeks after she had come, but even he heard nothing in his conversation with the good lady to enlighten everyone's curiosity. Captain Williams did his best to engage her in conversation, but her small talk was quite without effect. A second caller came enquiring after her and stayed but a short time. She was invited to the Rectory for a meal, but courteously declined the invitation. Then one morning she did not arrive in the rear parlour where she regularly partook of breakfast and a maid was dispatched to enquire if she would like breakfast to be served in her room. There was no response to the maid's knock and she returned to tell her mistress.

"Maybe she is tired and sleeping a little late. We'll wait a while and try again."

But there was no response. At noon Mrs Solent knocked and then entered the room calling Mrs Henrietta Benowith by name. But there lay the woman, stretched out on the bed, looking quite peaceful, but as the innkeeper's wife moved closer it was obvious that the woman was dead and there, at the side of her face, was a wet rag. Mrs Solent gasped, hurried from the room and down the stairs to her husband.

"Come, Jeremiah, quickly, the poor woman is dead!" Together they surveyed the scene. "Call the Rector; he will know what to do. It looks as though she has been dead these many hours, for she is cold and stiff. I'll get Jonathan Pierpoint, too, Jeremiah, for he will have to see to her. But don't touch anything till the Rector comes. We may need to call the law into this. There is something strange about this woman and now this."

The Rector came immediately and agreed that there was something strange about this affair. As he looked about the room his eye was caught by the damp cloth on the bed alongside the head and the wig, not entirely unusual, seemed to be well fastened onto the woman's head. From the disarrangement of the bedding it looked as if the woman had struggled before her death and that could point to other than natural causes. The Rector took Jeremiah aside and suggested that they send to Truro for the Magistrate. This was no ordinary death, of that the Rector was sure.

"Has anyone been visiting Mrs Benowith this morning?" the Rector asked.

"Not to my knowledge, for we were expecting her to come down to breakfast." Jonathan Peirpoint arrived and agreed that this was both unexpected and seemed strange that she had not called for help if she was ill in the night.

"But then it is strange that she should be fully dressed as though she had not been to bed, possibly dying last night."

"Yes, I agree," said the Rector thoughtfully. "However I think it well for you to remove the dear woman to your parlour Jonathan."

"Well, Rector that is most unusual, but I suppose we can go ahead with all the arrangements and one of those will be to trace her relatives up in London."

The Rector made a note of how the body had been found and the rag which to him, seemed to suggest that she had been asphyxiated.

"In that case she has been murdered! We certainly do need the Magistrate," he added.

The whole village was in an uproar of gossip as the news circulated and later that day the Magistrate arrived and was duly accommodated at The White Horses. He was invited to the Rectory for a meal and together with Jeremiah Solent discussed everything they could about the case. While they were in the midst of such, Jonathan Pierpoint arrived and burst in upon them in somewhat excited manner.

"Come in, come in, Jonathan, what is the matter that you seem so distressed?"

"Well, Rector, as you know it is my responsibility to attend, most intimately with such as are committed to my care. As I was preparing the body for lying in the casket, I discovered that Mrs Benowith is not a Mrs at all but a Mr!"

Chapter Seven

The Intrigue Deepens

That evening the parish council was to meet and the Rector thought it well to not cancel it, but use it to quell the gossip that was circulating like a wild fire around the village. Mrs Benowith had already become the chief subject of all and when the news got out that Mrs Benowith was really a Mr Benowith there was no limit to the speculation which the news ignited.

"Gentlemen," called the Rector as he brought the meeting to order. "We have a strange case on our hands. Strange indeed! How can I conduct a funeral of a woman who has lived for such a short time in our midst when that woman is really a man?"

"Rector," called old Joseph the chairman. "It seems to me that this woman ... man, has been living in disguise and Rector, you will beg my pardon, but you know something of that."

There was a ripple of laughter as the Rector acknowledged his part as smuggler of men from the Bastille not so many years before.

"Yes Joseph," replied the Rector. "My thoughts are simply that this woman...man, was living a lie for some not too good a purpose. Maybe she...he was in fear of her...his life." It was young John Prendegast who had recently come onto the Council, who questioned that if this was a case of murder, was it someone local who had committed the act or a visitor?

This brought a sobering silence upon them all.

"But surely there would have to be a motive for such a crime, and what could that be locally?" This was the wise comment of Jonathan Peirpoint. "Has anyone been questioned Rector?"

"As yet the magistrate has only surveyed the case from the evidence, but tomorrow he is going to listen to anything the maids and Captain Williams have to say."

"Rector," asked Donald Creedy with a glint of humour in his eye, "Captain Williams under suspicion seems a likely case, I'm sure! But he will enjoy being questioned."

The meeting settled down to church affairs and members were finally dismissed to their homes. The Rector spent a thoughtful night as he wondered just what this woman... man, had been hiding from.

With the morning came a meeting with the Magistrate in The White Horses and Captain Winton Willoughby Williams was smartly dressed for his stint under the searching questions of the magistrate.

"Sir, I understand that you are the only other resident living in here at the moment."

"Yes, Sir, and very comfortable I am, being a retired gentleman of His Majesty's regiments."

"Quite, quite," stammered the magistrate. "Where were you on the evening before this woman's... man's death?"

"Why I was here in this very parlour, Sir, and there are

many from the village that could vouch for me I'm sure," answered the Captain.

"Did you at any time leave the parlour and go upstairs during that time?"

"Oh no, Sir, I was here all evening enjoying the company of so many friends."

"Quite, quite."

"Oh, Sir," interjected the Captain. "I did leave the room just before supper. I had to fetch a clean kerchief ready for a little refreshment before retiring."

"So then," said the magistrate. "You must have passed by this woman's... man's... room and did you hear or see anything unusual and was there a light in the room?"

The Captain replied, "Oh I don't recall any signs of life or movement as I passed the door, but then the good lady...man, always sat in the front parlour of her apartment and I only passed the door leading into her bedroom."

"I see, I see," said the magistrate and offered the Captain the opportunity to leave the room. But he actually slipped into the corner and was keen to hear all the questioning.

The next young lady called was the maid who had several times knocked on the lady's door in the morning.

"Do I understand that you do not live in the premises young lady?"

"Oh, no Sir, only the master and mistress live in other than the guests of course."

"Quite, quite. Did you at any time before you left that evening see anyone go upstairs?"

"Oh yes, Sir, I saw Captain Williams go up very hurriedly just before we served his bread and cheese, he always needs a large handkerchief tucked into his shirt before he eats."

"Quite, quite! Have you anything you would like to tell us about this lady, gentleman?"

"Oh, no Sir, but I would like to tell you of something I noticed in Captain Williams' room the morning after this dreadful thing happened."

There was a stir in the room.

"And what was it that you saw?"

"Well, Sir, it was the lady's...man's necklace on Captain Williams' table, at the side of his bed."

There was a gasp from others in the room, but from the corner, a positive groan as if a cow were dying.

"Thank you, young lady; you may leave us a moment. I would ask Captain Williams to be called in again."

"He is already here your honour," the company said together and with great bluster Captain Williams struggled out of the corner to stand before the magistrate.

"Sir," said the magistrate, "you may please be seated and then perhaps you would be good enough to tell us how this necklace came to be in your possession on the day of this woman's... man's death?"

With a face as red as a cockerel's comb, the Captain struggled to compose his words to something of intelligent language, not without some difficulty. "Sir, when this dear lady... man, first came to stay I assured her that I would do anything I could to help her and make her stay comfortable. Well, on the afternoon of her...his, death, her necklace had broken as she tried to place it around her... his, neck. I saw her struggling with it and offered to repair it if it was broken. At first she refused to let me assist her... him, but finally gave up trying, and surrendered to my services. I took the necklace to my room, but could not fix it as I'd promised and was hoping to attend to it again in the following morning."

"Did you at any time enter the lady's... man's room to retrieve the necklace in order to effect the repair?" asked the magistrate.

"Oh no Sir, I took it from her here in this very room."

"And did anyone see you take it from her or hear you offer your services?"

"Oh no, Sir I was most discreet with the dear lady... man!"

"Thank you, you may leave, but I may need to speak to you again." To which the Magistrate added, "I think we shall refer to this woman...man as a person. I'm getting quite confused. Then I must ask my host and his dear lady a question or two. What understanding did you have with this person as to how long she...he would stay in your hostelry?"

"Well, we had no actual understanding, she...he paid us each week she was with us. She...he seemed to have all she needed money-wise, Sir. As to how long she would continue with us, she gave no indication and as we seldom have paying guests, it was not really a concern and we were happy to have her. She was certainly no trouble."

"Did she have many visitors during these weeks?" asked the Magistrate.

"To our knowledge she had but two men visitors who came and went within a matter of minutes. I must say we thought that strange, especially if they were relatives. She never ordered refreshment for them and to my knowledge they came and went on horseback. I am sure they hired them from Crendon Bywater, for I easily recognised their mounts as such as I have seen there at the Terapin. That's the inn on the quay at Crendon, Sir."

"And did she receive any letters at any time?"

"No, Sir, she... he seemed to be content not to have any

communication with the world outside Lower Penzle. She never mentioned more to us than that she hailed from Greenwich outside London and had a house near the Observatory, whatever that may be."

"Thank you, Master Solent. Perhaps we should retire now for lunch and I have some thoughts I would like to share with our good friend the Rector."

The company dispersed with a good deal of murmuring and even more suggestions to each other as to what this mystery was all about. The Magistrate, the Rector and Jonathan Peirpoint sat together around the fire and after some time of reflection the Rector made a suggestion."I rather think we should send someone to London to seek out a relative, otherwise we might not fulfil any requirements the family might have, if, that is our stranger has any to care about her death."

"Do you have any thoughts as to how we might find such, Rector?" asked the Magistrate.

"Well, I do know someone living south of the river in London and surely such a fashionable lady…sorry, gentleman, might be known and for that matter, missed these days she has been resident with us."

"Well, Rector," asked the Magistrate, "would you be prepared to make such a journey? It seems a lot to ask you for a perfect stranger whose reason for being here in disguise makes it all a mystery."

The Rector replied that he would need to have more information for his burial register if possible, so would look upon it as parish business. This settled, the Magistrate took his leave following a fine lunch at The White Horses fireside.

Chapter Eight

The London Connection

The Rector sat waiting outside the large impressive door of the Magistrate's office. Alongside him was Jack Dart, the Frenchman who had been so involved with the Rector's smuggling escapades. He had been the Rector's contact in London and they awaited an interview with the Greenwich Magistrate, hoping he could shed some light on this strange death. They were formally announced by the Magistrate's clerk and the gentleman himself eyed his visitors across the top of his tiny spectacles which seemed so precariously perched on the end of his nose that they promised to drop off as his face crinkled in a smile to greet them.

"And what may I have the pleasure of this visit for, gentlemen? I trust you have not brought me another case for the court tomorrow. It is already crowded and I fear anything further would have to be delayed."

"No, no, Sir, we have simply come in the hope that you could help us trace the relatives of a Mrs Henrietta Benowith who we believe may have had a residence in this parish."

"Oh dear, oh dear," intoned the Magistrate. "I fear you have brought me a further case for this woman's husband, and I was not aware that she had such, is being searched for all over London."

"Sir," broke in the Rector, "You should know that this Mrs Benowith is really a *Mr Benowith*."

"But you just said it was his wife, my good man. Please let us get this straight; this Mrs Benowith is really a *Mr Benowith*? Please explain what you mean!"

"I appreciate your being confused, for we who knew this woman were rightly also in a state of confusion, for she gave every indication by dress and jewellery that she was a perfectly respectable lady when she arrived and then for some weeks stayed at a hostelry in our village. But her death, and this we believe to be suspicious, caused us to discover that Mrs Henrietta Benowith was really Mr Benowith. Do I gather that someone of either sex is known to you, Sir?"

"Oh yes, you understand correctly. A Mr Henry Benowith was until a few weeks ago a respected official of the Greenwich Benevolent Bank. Then without any explanation, he disappeared from his home and business. We have since been informed that he took with him all the gold held in the bank's vaults, or at least we think he did, seeing they have gone as indeed he has gone. That is why I have issued a warrant for his arrest when found. But am I to understand that you have not only discovered this man masquerading as a woman and that she...he is now dead?"

"That is correct Sir, and we came seeking any relatives, and still do, that I may complete the arrangements for her...his burial." This was spoken by the Rector with some relief that his coming here had not been in vain.

"Sirs," said the Magistrate still shaking his head and still not quite losing his spectacles. "You must accompany me for lunch and we shall discuss what must be done."

Lunch was taken in a local inn and Jack Dart excused himself from the company and left the Rector to further investigate the possibilities of a relative being found. What now concerned the Magistrate was whether Mrs...Mr Benowith had with him the aforementioned gold.

"May I suggest that you approach the house of this man and as I am aware of a housekeeper looking after his affairs during his absence, she may be privy to where his personal effects are."

The Rector went straight to the address given and on the pretext of seeking his relatives, if any, he might be given some details which could be followed up.

"Oh, Sir, Mr Benowith gave strict, very strict instructions that I was not to answer any questions as he left in a great hurry, and I have now heard all the unkind gossip that has been told of him, gossip which I could never believe of the Master."

"I quite understand your loyalty, Madam, but I have the sad news to tell you that your master is dead." With this news the dear lady staggered back into the house, almost losing her balance and the Rector grasped her arm. In doing so he stood inside the hallway and from the rather gloomy interior a young man stepped forward.

"What's this you are saying? My uncle dead? But I saw him but a week ago and he was very much alive."

"Sir," said the Rector, "are you saying that you visited your uncle but a week ago at the White Horses Inn in Lower Penzle?"

"Yes, that I am and he was as well as you or I. What has ailed him?"

"Sir," continued the Rector, "If you saw your uncle then and you knew, as it seems many do that he was wanted by the Magistrates why did you not divulge his whereabouts?"

"I am not my brother's keeper good Sir. What is the law's business is the law's business and not mine. I also am an employee of the bank from which my uncle is supposed to have stolen gold. The whole story is, I believe, a smoke screen to hide some skulduggery within the governor's council."

"Then surely the quickest way to clear your uncle's name would be to bring him forward."

"I do not trust any of them, Sir, and I hope they will cease their accusations and seek the real criminal, if such has committed a crime."

"Then, Sir, may I ask you to accompany me back to my parish and allow me to conduct a decent burial of your uncle?"

"Indeed I will do that and I am obliged to you for the invitation."

Arrangements were made that on the following day they would set out for Plymouth and Lower Penzle.

But that evening the Rector dined with the Magistrate and divulged all he had discovered from the nephew. The Magistrate was surprised to hear that such a nephew actually worked for the bank and as they talked, the Rector became more and more suspicious that this nephew may not be such as he had not mentioned the disguise the uncle was hiding under. However, the two men boarded the coach for the South West and had little conversation as they sat atop the coach most of the way, there being little room within for other than the ladies travelling. They stopped and lodged at one inn after another, sometimes stopping just for meals and then on down the Avon Valley to Bath, across the Mendip Hills to Taunton and then to Exeter. There they boarded the Plymouth coach and then on to Truro and finally down the final stretch to Lower Penzle. The Rector watched carefully the behaviour of his companion, for he made no attempt to take down his bags and even said to the coachman, "How much further to Lower Penzle?"

"Why, Sir, you're there!" This made the Rector more sure than ever that this young man was not who he said he was.

He took him inside and directly whispered to Jeremiah to take the young man up to the very room where his 'uncle' had died and to watch his reaction. There was none and his every action seemed to underline that he had never before been to the inn. Before he had even taken his travel coat off, he asked the host, "Where are my uncle's effects?"

Jeremiah answered, "Oh I've got them safely put away. There are few indeed, though his trunk is a fair weight, I must say."

The young man demanded, "I would be glad to inspect them as soon as possible."

"Oh, I'm sure after such a long journey you will be requiring a meal."

"Yes, of course, but I still would like to inspect the trunk before I retire!"

The Rector stood just outside the door as this conversation was held and down in the parlour he asked the landlord if he had himself seen the contents of the trunk.

"Indeed I have not Rector, for we do not have a key!"

"Ho, ho! That will be interesting my friend. We shall see if this young man has any reason for us not seeing the contents of the trunk!"

"Are you suspicious Rector? Do you think there could be the stolen gold hidden there?"

"Maybe, maybe, Jeremiah, we shall see in the morning how he intends to behave regarding the trunk."

The Rector had sent word for the Truro Magistrate to be present at the inn and so as the Rector, Jeremiah and the Magistrate met with the 'nephew' they awaited his reaction when he was informed that no one there had a key to inspect the contents. To their surprise the 'nephew' never turned a hair but even seemed pleased that his 'uncle's' personal effects were not to be disturbed.

"I'll take the trunk as it is and his housekeeper will deal with the clothes of my uncle."

"But, good Sir, we would need some clear identity to let you take the trunk away seeing there is such suspicion on this whole affair." This was spoken by the Truro Magistrate and the young man seemed undeterred by this prohibition. It was then that he dropped a further surprise into the conversation.

"Sirs, you had better know that I am not this man's nephew, but an employee of the bank's trustees and employed by them to trace the stolen gold."

"That explains then why I have suspected that you did not, indeed visit your 'uncle' here before."

"That is correct Rector, all I am here for is to seek to recover the gold. What is to be done concerning the deceased is your affair."

"Indeed," said the Rector, "it is our affair, for we have on our hands a possible murder as well as a thief."

The trunk was duly brought to them and after some attention by the undertaker was opened. There with a few women's clothes, a wig and jewellery was the stolen gold. The Magistrate was satisfied that the young man was indeed employed by the bank and with a soldier to accompany him back to London was allowed to leave Lower Penzle to clear up the rest of the mystery of Mrs...Mr Benowith.

Life in the village settled down to its normal peaceful rhythm and the Rector began to think that perhaps he had allowed his imagination to believe a murder had been committed, when it was really an unfortunate end to a thief in hiding. However, a stranger arrived at The White Horses a few days after the funeral had taken place of the mysterious Mrs...Mr Benowith, asking what had become of the personal effects of the deceased. The man seemed shocked that someone had been from London to collect such and claimed to be very indignant that all had been settled so hurriedly. The Rector was informed of his presence and came into the inn to answer his questions.

"And who, may I ask are you, my friend, and how did you hear of the death?"

"Oh I have only now heard of it, Sir, I came to visit Mrs Benowith, as I have before."

"Oh," said the Rector, "So you were the unknown visitor some weeks back?"

"Yes, and I am rather shocked to hear that the bank has collected her personal effects so soon. How, indeed, did they know of her passing?"

"That, my friend, was because I travelled to London to find any relative, not aware that you were somewhere hereabouts."

"Oh, I was simply aware of Mrs Benowith's presence and desired to know of her wellbeing. Now that she is dead, I must travel back to London, saddened that I could not even pay my last respects for the dear lady."

"I'm afraid, friend, that I must ask you to await a while,

as we may need some answers to the mystery of this lady."

"Oh, I cannot hinder from leaving this very day Sir, I must bear the news of her death to her relatives which you apparently have not traced."

The Rector gripped the man's arm and helped him be seated, much to his displeasure, as in walked the Truro Magistrate.

"Sir," said the new arrival, "I take it you were well acquainted with Mrs Benowith?"

"Oh yes, we were old friends of many years."

"Then how come you know her as Mrs Benowith when we have found that she is rather a man in disguise?"

"I don't know what you are talking about. Mrs Benowith was here and I visited her here. Everyone here saw her and how can you say she was anything but Mrs Benowith?"

The Magistrate then asked the stranger, "When did you last visit the deceased?"

"Oh, it must have been some two weeks since. It was late one evening when the inn was very busy. I made my way up to her rooms without passing through the parlour."

"And," asked the Magistrate, "was the deceased well?"

"Oh yes! In fact she arranged that I should visit her today."

"Then, Sir, I have to inform you that you are under serious suspicion of murder."

"What?"

"Yes, Sir, for you are obviously aware of the deceased's disguise and reason for being here. You freely admit to visiting her unknown to the host here at the White Horses and now come hoping to obtain her personal effects, which we have reason to believe contained nothing less that gold stolen from the London Bank."

With this the man changed colour and made to stand.

He was immediately pushed back onto his chair and the Magistrate gave word for him to be transported to Truro.

"Rector, I have to thank you for uncovering this whole affair. It seems that your days of adventure are not over. Who knows what next will take place in Lower Penzle? I am much obliged to you!"

The afternoon rides across the cliff tops were not wholly at an end for the Rector and his wife, but following the birth of John Henry a trap had been purchased and this afternoon the three sat comfortably trotting up the hill to Henry Gritton's mill. For some time the pair chatted in lively conversation, when Alicia posed a question of the Rector.

"John, how was the young man finally convicted of the murder? It seemed to me purely circumstantial evidence that put him in the picture. It could have been any time that he had visited Mrs Benowith."

"Ah, that is where our friend Captain Winton Willoughby Williams came in. He was, as you may expect, sitting prominently in the court hearing. When the piece of muslin rag was called as evidence of the murder weapon, our friend suddenly rose to his feet, coughed and rushed forward to the front of the court. There was a flurry of activity as he asked to speak to the Judge and after a somewhat confused moment he was ushered into the witness box by the clerk at the request of the prosecution. The accused was defending himself and although he objected, his objection was overruled by the Judge and Captain Williams stood waiting to be sworn in. With some pomposity he took the oath and with a slight bow he addressed the court. "Your honour and members of the court, I am a captain of the King's forces now retired and resident in a most comfortable accommodation at The White Horses Inn in Lower Penzle. I am also now an esteemed member of the community having been sexton of the... "And here he was interrupted by the Judge. "Captain Willoughby or whatever your name is, we do not require a history or pedigree. I have given you permission to state your evidence against the accused. Will you please get on with it." "The name is Williams, your honour, Winton Willoughby Williams." "I do not care if it is Lucifer, man; just get on with your evidence!" "Yes your honour! Well, I was not aware that I could help in this case until now, but being an officer of the King and observant as such, I must state that until now I was not remembering much about the night of this happening until this piece of muslin cloth was shown. You see I had to leave the parlour of the said White Horses Inn to fetch a clean kerchief to prepare for my supper refreshment. I always use a clean kerchief, your honour, having care for my uniform when not in retirement." "Yes, yes, yes, man, kindly get on with it." "Well, as I left the parlour to go upstairs, my room is right at the top, I passed the accused, though until now I did not recognise him. But on that occasion he was wearing a bandana around his head and I thought he was just one of the seamen, although not a Lower Penzle man. But I recognise that muslin cloth as its coloured line ran right around the man's head." "Thank you officer!" "Oh, it is a pleasure to be of assistance your Honour, I'm sure!" "Captain you may stand down." "Thank you, thank you, your honour."

"So that was what clinched the whole affair," said Alicia. "Fancy our dear old Captain Williams being the final link in the chain. Will the man hang, John?"

"I expect he will unless he is deported, which may well

be, seeing the murdered man was himself guilty of a crime. But I don't think we have heard the last of this with Captain Williams in the front line."

"But maybe we will have a little quietness in Lower Penzle," said Henry Gritton as they enjoyed their tea together at the mill.

"I for one would be happy for that, and I think young John Henry here would like to grow up in a law-abiding community too," concluded the Rector.

The Rector of Lower Penzle

Chapter Nine

The Way to a Man's Heart

"Oh Captain, how very brave you are to stand and give evidence against a murderer!"

"Come, come Ma'm, I did but do my duty whatever the consequences might be. After all the man is in custody and will probably go to the gallows."

This was the conversation going on in Widow Adams kitchen before a meal was served to the brave Captain W. W. Williams. His statement at the Truro Court had been largely reported with no doubt embellishments ever since the trial for the murder of Mrs...Mr Benowith at The White Horses Inn. The Rector was looked upon as the brains behind the capture and conviction, whilst Captain Williams had but put the lid on it all.

Widow Adams bade Captain Williams sit himself down although he was already there, sitting with the large, white handkerchief firmly tucked into his collar. His posture was that of a babe in a high chair and his hold of knife and fork, whilst not in the true rolls of etiquette, was as it were arms at the ready for attack! A large steak and kidney pie was the emplacement to be captured and Widow Adams apologised that it seemed so large.

"Ma'm, do not be anxious that any will be wasted or even left for the birds. We shall do this meal proud and of that you may be sure."

Although Captain Williams had taken on board a good deal of religion when preparing himself to be parish sexton, he did not see why time should be wasted thanking God for what his appetite was about to surely show as he tucked into his serving. And he would feel he had been most unthankful both to God and Widow Adams if he did not accept both the first and second helping.

Following the meal he was really ready to retire, but Widow Adams was ready to have her meal companion sit and chat over all the events of the day, week or year. The Captain, carefully at first and then a little later, hid his tiredness from view as a yawn would follow yawn and even an occasional snort as his eyelids lowered from time to time. It was on one of these occasions that Widow Adams made bold to say that Captain Williams should seriously consider his loneliness as a single professional man.

"Ma'm," spluttered Captain Williams as he suddenly realised what she was saying and the way the conversation had wandered without him realising it. "Madam, I have considered my position often and never more than when I have been in your presence and under the influence of such wonderful culinary delights as that steak and kidney pie!"

"Then Sir, why don't you do something about it and make your future appetite secure!"

"Ma'm, are you suggesting what I think you are suggesting?" The Captain was now fully awake and breathing large amounts of air.

"I am, but stating what I have felt so often in your

company that it was high time Mr Adams was replaced in my memory with a living companion who could do justice to my gifts."

"Then Ma'm, we should surely consider the seriousness of such a proposal especially seeing it is not a Leap Year!"

"Oh, why bless your heart Sir, I am not making the proposal, but seeking your advice."

Now the Captain began to be confused. Had Widow Adams not made at least an inferential proposal of marriage, or was he perhaps reading into her statement too much? What was he to do, carry on this conversation or stop it before he had committed himself?

"Well, well, if you feel you could not trust that my culinary efforts would not satisfy your deepest needs Captain. I know there are others who view your good self as being very eligible. But I am not sure they could look after your needs as I could, and I'm not wishing to boast."

"Ma'm, you could never boast beyond what I know all too well are your culinary gifts. No woman could ever match you nor compare with your ministry to your humble servant."

"Then I take it you feel happy to move from a simple visitor to a resident at some stage in the not too distant future."

"Ma'm, you leave me with no room to retreat, if I wished to and that I feel I do not wish to. But I could not consider a change in my accommodation other than in a married state."

"Sir," shrieked the widow, "I was not suggesting other."

"God help us, no Ma'm. I was not suggesting other myself."

"Then it is settled and I may leave you to see the Rector in your good time."

"I...I will indeed," said the Captain taking a deep breath as he realised just what a steak and kidney pie had led him into.

"And not a moment too soon, Captain," said the Rector when the next day the Captain attended upon him with the request.

Mrs Jones heard his stuttering request of the Rector and chuckled to herself as she wondered if Widow Adams was taking on more than she bargained for in husband number four. News travelled round the village and Captain Williams blushed and stammered as he was congratulated on Sunday as he gathered in the vestry and later stood at the door with the Rector.

All awaited the great day and when it arrived Widow Adams was arrayed in a fine new dress and a bonnet fit for a queen. The Captain wore his uniform, having gained permission from the commandant of the regiment in Truro. Of all the guests none was as bold as Sergeant Sigrose, his tall lean figure and oversized uniform hung on him as if no one was inside, but he was evidently thrilled that at last the Captain had someone to care for his culinary needs. He was however wary of how long Widow Adams' fourth marriage would last, not through neglect, but rather through a surplus of care served beneath a pie crust.

As the bells rang out the ringers pulled their heartiest in memory of the Captain's midnight escapade as he set the bells ringing at that time when he entered the bell tower to watch for the smugglers. Their effort did not go unobserved by the Captain himself.

The Rector and Alicia sat enjoying the firelight glow before lighting the lamps and held hands as they thought of the Captain and his new bride settling into Widow Adams', now Mrs Williams' cottage.

"Surely the church will be able and willing to purchase a larger cassock for our sexton, don't you think?"

"Well, with all those pies and so little walking to obtain them Captain Williams will certainly not fit into that uniform again, that's for sure!"

It was church matters which soon occupied the Rector's attention as across the county crowds were to gather at Gwennap Pit, a natural amphitheatre, there to hear the preaching of John Wesley. Three hundred tin miners and their families were gathered, singing and praying, among them Henry Gritton, having left his mill for some days in the hands of a farm hand not interested in Henry's spiritual pursuits. The Rector usually ignored such meetings as those now being held across on the north corner of the county, but members of his parish council had been attracted and his own curiosity caused him to take Alicia in the trap to hear this member of the Anglican ministry who felt willing to disobey the bishops and preach wherever crowds were willing to listen.

Further east in Bristol George Whitefield had found a great following among the miners and now news had spread to the very end of the kingdom as Wesley rode from place to place ministering to his societies. The Rector was concerned about his own flock's well being under these new emotional influences. He was determined to taste Wesley for himself and make a judgement first hand. The crowds gathered and after some stirring singing of songs strange to John Trevethin, but pleasing to his musical taste, the great man himself stood up and with a piercing voice preached to several hundred. Following the preaching men and women gathered in groups to pray and the Rector found himself and Alicia among a small group earnestly praying for their own souls and for their friends and neighbours not present. The Rector was deeply moved and after a while, taking Alicia by the hand, he moved out of the crowd to where they had left their trap. It was a long journey back across the county, so they did not tarry. Their conversation was serious and John Trevethin found himself challenged by all he had seen and heard. But he was also troubled as to how this would affect his parish and those especially of his parish council whom he had seen in the crowd. His conviction that these Methodists were right in their theology, but dangerously divisive in their churchmanship, caused him to wonder how things might change.

The next parish council meeting met and before local business was discussed old Joseph Trenbeath asked if he might say something on behalf of those who had attended the Gwennap.

"Rector, you will know that some of us made the journey which you yourself made to hear the Rev John Wesley. We were all greatly moved and challenged in our lives by what we heard, but we want to say that nothing we heard, or felt in that gathering, made us want to join the dissenters calling themselves Methodists after their leader's strict methods of living. While we feel deeply our need to follow the truths of the church, we want you to know that we stand squarely in our churchmanship with you."

There was a series of what sounded like softly breathed "amens" uttered by all in the room. To this speech the Rector quietly stood to his feet and in a warm, but formal way addressed those gathered round the room, a room which had seen a great deal of brotherhood and loyalty over the years of smuggling, danger and humour.

"Gentlemen, I came here tonight with a heavy heart, seriously wondering what effect your attendance at

Gwennap had upon you all. I personally was deeply moved and challenged as to my preaching and teaching as a parish priest responsible for your souls. I had strong fears however that these deep feelings which obviously you experienced, too, would lead to dissension amongst us. You know of my strong friendship with miller Gritton and my admiration for his stand on Christian morals and simplicity of worship. Well, now you have spoken I am relieved and encouraged to feel that we can follow our consciences and continue to worship according to our traditions with deep sincerity and love for our common Lord, whatever we may be labelled. I would like to propose that we invite miller Gritton to join us if he so desires, for he shares with us so much and not the least it was he who brought to me the love of my life."

At this there was almost a cheer across the room. And as if by order, the door opened and in came Alicia and Mrs Jones with the usual ample refreshment of the evening.

"I think," said Joseph, "If we were Methodists we would call this a 'Love Feast', and that would be a true description, what say all of you?"

The Rector of Lower Penzle

Chapter Ten

Mystery from the Mists

All month sea mists had hung over the south coast of Cornwall and everyone longed for the sun to disperse them. Lamps had been lit in many homes burning precious oil usually lasting the winter. Even walking proved a hazard at times as folk stumbled along suddenly appearing to each other and then disappearing as quickly. Into the gloom rode a company of some ten soldiers, visiting first The White Horses inn and then the church, making their way up the hill to the rectory. There their officer dismounted and demanded to speak to the Rector. Mrs Jones, shocked by the sense of urgency in his demand, called the Rector from his study.

"Come in, Sir, and tell me what you are about in this wretched weather. It has not lifted for weeks and one wonders if it will ever."

"You are right," replied the officer. "We are on the search for an escaped prisoner from Launceston Jail."

"Well, you don't tell me that Master George Fox has escaped and is holding some forbidden meetings hereabouts?"

"N...no, I wish it were just he, for we could leave him to preach until the weather clears. No, this man was being transferred to the new hulks that are stationed on the Tamar, when he slipped his guard and will be probably seeking a sea escape we think. So I'm asking all your parishioners to keep a vigilant lookout for him. He's both dangerous and desperate."

"Well, thank you for warning us officer, there are no sea going vessels using our little harbour these days, but further up the coast at Crendon Bywater the *Sea Winkle* is a regular coastal and cross channel voyager."

"Aye Sir, we are aware of that, but it's hardly likely that our man will take a recognised ship. He was due to be deported, so me thinks he might deport himself and save us the trouble."

"You may be right, Sir."

With that the company galloped away down to the village and the Rector was left to explain to Mrs Jones and Alicia what they had not already heard.

"It will be as well to stay in during darkness ladies and especially don't let John Henry out in the garden till this mist clears, though I fear it may be days yet."

The Rector was right for the mist hung for several more days, making every footstep suspicious as one heard it behind one when walking about the village.

On Sunday candles were lit even for the morning service and by evening few ventured out to Evensong. The Rector made his way home from that service glad to see a fire burning in the hallway. He took off his cloak and made his way into the sitting room only to find Alicia and Mrs Jones sitting without a movement or a word of welcome. They looked straight at him, but didn't say a word.

"Just come in Rector and sit over there!" The voice that gave these orders was strange and quietly spoken. The Rector knew immediately that this must be the escapee from Launceston and had come to the Rectory while he was at service. He looked around the room and there seated in an armchair behind the door was a man dressed not in prison garb but somewhat smartly clothed, if a little dishevelled.

"I take it you are our friend from Launceston, Sir? You are expected."

"And who is expecting me, Sir, unless you mean His Majesty's men at arms?"

"You are right there my man, but to my knowledge they are not here to welcome you and we are not likely to be a danger to you, so let my wife and housekeeper get us some refreshment."

"That is kind of you and very welcome. But I cannot risk them running from the house, so where they go, we all go together and food sounds good to me on this misty night."

The visitor held a dangerous looking dagger in his hand as he ordered them to stand and walk into the kitchen.

"And I warn you that if anyone attempts to leave the house someone here will get seriously hurt. I am already accused of murder, and although innocent, will not hesitate to wound if I need to. And remember there is a small child upstairs you tell me, so he would not wish to be without a mother, would he?"

"Sir," said the Rector as calmly as he could, "you need fear nothing from us and we would be glad to know your case and how you could be incarcerated if innocent."

Together they stood and with the dagger held close by Alicia's back, they processed into the kitchen. They had not been there more than ten minutes when a movement was heard in the hallway.

"Stand still and stay quiet, said the convict as the kitchen door slowly opened and a sleepy eyed young boy dragging his blanket stumbled in upon the hostages.

"What's going on, Daddy? Are you playing a game?"

"Come in and be very quiet son, this gentleman is needing some food, so come and sit down and you can have some, too."

"You mean I don't have to go back to bed? I like this game!"

They all gave a weak laugh and encouraged him to simply play along. Food was soon made ready and they all ate standing around the kitchen until all had had what they felt able to eat and then they processed back, not to the sitting room, but to the study. This was where the Rector led them and the convict hardly seemed to realise that they had been led to another room. Alicia realised that her husband was working out a plan and she smiled at him knowingly. He did not respond, but quietly walked in and sat at his desk.

Only when the convict realised the different room did he ask why they had changed rooms.

"Well," said the Rector, "if anyone was to come tonight to see me they would think it strange that I was not in my study."

"I warn you Rector, if you are planning something, I will not hesitate to inflict a wound and who would want such to be done in front of your son?"

"Right, right, but surely we are not expected to remain here sitting up all night and how will that help your escape?"

"When I am ready to leave I will lock you into this

room, for I notice there is a key in the lock, and then when I've saddled your horse and made ready to leave I'll unlock the door and you will be unharmed and free to go and tell who you like. Do you understand? But no funny business or I won't hesitate to do the worst."

With this he turned, left the room, and they heard him lock the door and take the key.

"Quick all of you, come over here." The Rector stood by his bookcase and flicking his finger under the shelf he released the lock and swung the book case open. Not a word was spoken as each of them filed into the tunnel staircase and out of the room. The Rector swung the case closed and tripped the lock. Then he told them all to feel their way down the stairs and slowly along the old tunnel. He hoped that with age and disuse no fall had taken place. He however stayed to hear what happened if the convict came back into the study and saw there was no one there. After a while he heard the convict tread through the hall and unlock the door. He peered into the room and whistled.

"Where have they gone? How did they get out of this room?"

He crossed over to the window, fully expecting it still to be open, but it was soundly closed and the shutters still tightly closed, too.

"What kind of a house is this? Can there be a secret door somewhere? Shall I waste time hunting for it? Better make my getaway!"

As soon as the Rector was aware that the horse had cantered away from the front of the Rectory, he called to his family not to go further along the tunnel, but to come back to the staircase. The convict galloped away to the high road and was lost in the swirling mist and darkness of the night. Leaving the family safely in the house, the

Rector rode Alicia's horse down to the village, hoping that the convict had gone up to the high road. It had been a hair raising experience for them all, now he felt a need to somehow get word to the soldiers that their quarry was indeed still in the county and seemingly not making for the sea. Little did he know that what he had experienced, his friend, the captain of the *Sea Winkle* was about to know, too well, as the convict turned from the high road down into Crendon Bywater and the harbour side tavern. Making fast his horse, he stealthily entered the small bar room and made as though stranded in the mist, he needed some food. The one thing he needed was a pistol and where better than on board a ship where such would be kept under lock and key against mutiny or some such rebellion. How could he find the master of this old lugger of a craft tied up at the quay?

He surveyed the few men around the room and considered one was perhaps that master. If he could find some excuse to get him outside he could enquire as to his next sailing or just show an interest in the old ship. But on such a night of mist and darkness he knew he had no chance. He must await the morning.

"I'm thoroughly lost in these parts, I wonder if landlord you could find a bed for me this night? I will hope this mist clears by daylight!"

The landlord eyed his customer, as did all in the room. "Where are you making for, friend?"

"Oh just as far as Plymouth. I have business with a fishing smack whose owner I have trade with for my trade in Launceston."

"Oh well, friend, we can surely make up a bed for the one night, I'm sure."

And with this he disappeared and ordered his wife to

make such ready for a visitor. No sooner had the visitor retired to bed than a horse was heard outside the *Terrapin Inn* and after a while the door opened and the Rector of Lower Penzle entered, warily as though he was expecting to see someone in the tavern's bar room. He looked round furtively and one of the late drinkers, knowing the Rector asked if he was expecting to see someone.

"Aye! That is exactly what I was expecting, as I see my own horse tied up where I've tied my wife's mare. Has the rider left or is he still about?"

"Oh, he's staying the night Rector, so you'll find him up the stair."

"Hush, man, I don't want him to know that I am here. He is the convict the troops are searching for and I've already had an unpleasant experience of him. No, I will ride to Crendon Hall and inform them that the man they search for is here."

By this time the landlord had appeared and hearing what the Rector had said, stated that he wondered himself if he had someone under his roof who ought to be residing at the King's pleasure somewhere else.

"Indeed he should, so kindly keep my visit quiet and I'll be off to Crendon Hall."

While they were talking their visitor had been listening above the stair and now, alerted to his own danger of being trapped, he decided now was the time to act and act without anyone downstairs knowing he had gone. Climbing from his window into the back yard of the inn, he crept out along the quay to where the *Sea Winkle* was moored and surveyed its ropes and sails. He might just be able to manage its navigation alone if he could drop the sail and get her out on the open sea. Silently, he stepped aboard and in the darkness felt along the deck to the mast.

There he felt up it to where the sail was tethered and with his dagger cut through the ropes and felt the sail drop on its beam. He then got back off the deck and pushed with all his strength to ease the *Sea Winkle* away from the quay and felt her begin to move gently as her sail filled a little with such wind as there was. Jumping back on board he grabbed the wheel and held it hard over until the prow pointed out to the harbour entrance. All seemed to be going well and no one seemed to stir on the quay. He had never handled a boat in his life, but he was determined whatever to get this old tub out on the sea and sail due south if he could but tether the beam and allow the wind to fill the sail.

The Rector arrived at a sleeping Crendon Hall and after a while raised the servants to answer his bell pull. Sir Richard was called and soon it seemed the whole household was awake as the Rector told of his find.

"I'm sorry to say the military left early today Rector, they were to camp on the moor tonight and continue their search tomorrow."

"Thank you sir, I will search for them tonight and maybe I can catch up with them before our quarry escapes further."

With this he took his leave and rode alone out over the headland to the moor, hoping he might see a fire or some sign of where the military were camping.

Out in the bay the mist enveloped the *Sea Winkle*, but also denied it the wind it so desperately needed to get it away out to sea. The convict pushed the beam first to one side then to the other without much success in finding wind enough to get her underway. He cursed the weather which while hiding his vessel from the land also denied him the means to make headway. He could just make out a little wake behind the ship and persuaded himself that he was progressing a little away from the land, but with no stars to be seen he hardly knew which way he was moving, even if it was a painfully slow movement. He looked at the compass ahead of the wheel and saw he was indeed sailing south. He neither knew to pray for the mist to rise and give him some wind nor to pray for its staying to hide his vessel from any who would surely give chase. He found an old cloak in the cabin and wrapped it around his shoulders as the cold damp mist seemed to wrap itself around him in clammy cold wetting him through. It was the cold that reminded him that he had ordered a hot tankard of rum to be taken to his room. How foolish that had been. They would now know that he had escaped. How long would it be before someone saw the *Sea Winkle* was missing and alerted Captain Storeton that his faithful old bark had been stolen?

Up on the moor, the Rector was ready to give up on his attempt to find the King's men. The mist prevailed and no matter how well he knew the moor, he still had no idea where they might be. But then a dim light ahead alerted him to someone's presence and then he heard voices. Yes, this must be the camping King's men. They welcomed him and heard gladly of his find, sympathising with him concerning the dangerous experience he and his family had been through. Orders were given and within a short while the camp was broken and they all moved off with the Rector back to Crendon Bywater. But to their dismay the bird had flown and no one seemed to know where or how, for the Rector's horse was still tethered in the yard of the *Terrapin*. It was only as day broke that someone noticed that the *Sea Winkle* was not at her moorings.

"I guess Captain Storeton has been hijacked to take the man off."

But they soon found that Captain Storeton was still in his house!

Horrified, he was soon dressed and went to his moorings to inspect the ropes. They had been cast off as would be expected, but how did this man manage to get the *Sea Winkle* to sea alone?

"It would be possible," said the Captain, "but it would be near impossible to sail her if there was a sea running, which of course there is not, and with this mist there is hardly any wind, so he cannot have got far."

What the Captain did not know was that as the convict in his ship sailed away from the coast the mist had cleared a little with an offshore wind and the old vessel was making a fair headway due south, moving with the tide she was taking her helmsman a little to the east.

"What other vessel is there in the harbour that we can get under sail, Captain?" asked the officer in charge of his company.

"I'm afraid there isn't a sea-going vessel apart from the *Sea Winkle*, Sir, but if we man a gig we might get out to sea, but with this mist, what hope have we in finding him?"

"But," said the Rector, "he cannot have gone all that far with so little wind!"

"That's right Rector, so we could take a couple of boats and row out to the south and east. I cannot just sit here and know my old faithful is sailing under a convict flag! Right then, let's make up two crews with some of your men, officer, and some men who are used to the sea, for we will need good rowers."

The officer sought out his likely men and Captain Storeton and the Rector took a boat each. Keeping within hailing distance they rowed out of the harbour into the mist.

Mystery from the Mists

On board the *Sea Winkle* the convict was having a time trying to control the beam as it swung in the wind, first one way and then another. But he somehow managed to hold the old ship steadily on a southerly course even though the tidal forces of the channel carried him to the east. The little he knew of the geography of the region made him aware that the first land he could hope for would be the Channel Isles. As the wind freshened and his speed increased, he anticipated escaping at least as far as these lands and from there he could no doubt get to France. Whilst the wind helped him, it hindered the rowers who toiled through the mist and out into the windswept channel where both boats made heavy weather of their rowing, so much so that the officer was all for turning back. Captain Storeton in one boat and the Rector in the other would have none of it. The *Sea Winkle* would surely be sighted if they kept rowing to the south. They also were being carried east by the tidal currents, so although they did not know it, they were following in the exact course of the *Sea Winkle* even though she had found her wind filled sails aiding her convict captain on his way to freedom.

The rowers tired and now windswept struggled on and eventually found themselves heading for Guernsey. No sign of the *Sea Winkle* until they rounded the headland and rowed into St Peter Port. There they asked concerning any sighting of their quarry and heard fishermen speak of seeing a bark of their description sailing with a rather awkward sail set and passing between St Peter Port and the small island of Sark. Tired as they were both the Rector and the officer and Captain Storeton decided to row out again. Sailing due south according to Captain Storeton's guidance they pulled on until they saw Jersey ahead of them. They decided to separate and as one boat rowed east of Jersey the other rowed west feeling they may even catch sight of the *Sea Winkle* making for France.

After some strong currents were negotiated on the eastern side of Jersey they saw their quarry beached on a sand bar near a dangerous outcrop of rock. As Captain Storeton's boat joined them they drew into the sheltered water and beached both their boats alongside the *Sea Winkle*. Climbing aboard they found it empty and Captain Storeton and his men pulled down the sail and ran out an anchor. They would refloat *Sea Winkle* on the next tide, but the officer begged them to await the capture of their man so that they may ferry him back to justice. The officer and his men made their way up the rocks and onto the headland. They felt they had some chance of a sighting or at least if they contacted the island folk they could get help to search. And so it was that they moved onto the rough cart tracks of the island and calling on such houses as they came to they asked of a stranger and it was not long before they found themselves obviously on his tracks. But as time went on it seemed he eluded their search.

The Captain and the Rector stayed on the shore, only climbing the headland when some islanders offered them some refreshment. They were more than ready for whatever was offered and the Rector spoke of his desire to get back to Cornwall as soon as possible.

"Well, I suggest we use the next tide to refloat the old lady and set off home whether or not our friend is found," said the Captain. This was readily agreed by the few who had not been included in the search party, not being armed men.

Leaving the two gigs well above high water, *Sea Winkle* lifted herself off the sand and slowly responded to the wind in her properly set sail, turned and made for home. As they passed along the south and then the west coast of the island they saw and signalled to the officer and his men and were waved on their way. If the fugitive was ever found and when the officer and men returned to England, no one seemed to know but once again Lower Penzle settled to a quieter life again and enjoyed its Rector's pastoral care and his wife's beauty as one by one she nurtured her little family and sat most prettily each Sunday in the Rector's pew.

The Rector of Lower Penzle

Chapter Eleven

Nero's Recital at the Mill

One of the ambitions the Rector had for his children was that they love music as much as he did. Alicia was in whole hearted agreement and carefully encouraged John Henry to keep at his practice and try his best to master his instrument, the violin. This was his father's choice as John himself played it well. So well that when George Fredrick Handel's new oratorio was to be performed at Truro Cathedral, the Rector was called upon to join the newly formed orchestra. Each week the trap set off with its passengers on the road to Truro and each week John arrived home in the early hours of the morning, tired, but jubilant as he mused upon the fine music of *The Messiah*. This was a superb and inspiring musical exercise for one who had so little opportunity to hear recitals of a professional nature in the rugged wiles of the Cornish coastland.

Finally, the day of the recital came and John, Alicia and John Henry set off early in the morning. On the High Road they fell in with several other parishioners and Henry Gritton and his wife from the mill. It was a rare occasion and there was an air of great anticipation in every cart and wagon as they exchanged comments in passing one another, or stopping for refreshments by the wayside. This was not only an opportunity for John Trevethin to exercise his gift in music, but for the first time John Henry was going to be allowed to play alongside his father in a few parts he had practiced so hard to achieve. Finally, they arrived at the great cathedral and as they tethered their horses in the yards of inns and some private houses, they moved into the cathedral itself to see the stands that had been set up for both orchestra and choir. The atmosphere was charged with expectation and nervous anticipation. Handel himself may not be present, but everyone was set to perform this lovely oratorio to the best of their ability.

Some sat outside the cathedral to eat their food, while others visited the local hostelries to rest and prepare for the evening's performance. Finally, as the time approached a call went out for choir and orchestra to find their places and all was ready for the conductor's baton to be raised. John and John Henry sat side by side and the Rector pointed to the part of the score John Henry was to join in. The conductor eyed the young player with a quizzical frown, but the Rector nodded and so the great sounds of the strings moved majestically into the first movement. The choir came in and soloists kept pace with the timing as the whole oratorio moved through piece after piece until a break was made and all relaxed and a hum of conversation spread across the great nave. Then the serious notes of *He was despised* brought everyone to the quietness of serious contemplation. The whole congregation felt the thrill of the *Hallelujah Chorus* and came eventually to the great notes of the question, *Oh Death Where is Thy Sting?* As the last notes died a great silence swept across the nave and then as if released by some unseen hand all began to talk of their admiration for both the composer and their own efforts to perform this great musical experience. John, John Henry and Alicia joined others of their parish and slowly made their way out into the darkened street of the city to find their traps and carts, wagons and horses for the long trek home.

Henry Gritton was as pleased as any to have witnessed his little niece's son actually performing with an orchestra. All the hours of practice had proved to be worthwhile and Henry looked upon the lad as if he were his grandson, over and over again he called across from his wagon his congratulations, till the little lad was embarrassed and finally fell asleep leaning on his mother's arms.

It was well on into the early hours that the parishioners of Lower Penzle came over the hill and began to descend on the road down from the moor. They all saw it at the same time and a cry went up. "There's something afire beyond the village!" But it was Henry that recognised just where the fire must be. It was beyond the village on the hill and then all realised the dreaded truth. It was the mill! Henry shouted his recognition and all joined in his cry of despair. As they came nearer they saw the whole mill burning like a torch, its sails each adding a grotesque effect as though they were hands held up for help. Flames shot high and from time to time sparks shot heavenward as another part collapsed into the inferno. It mattered not how much they all hurried their wagons and traps along, the mill was gone and nothing could save the grand old lady from her fiery fate. Someone, not meaning to be facetious called, "It seems we were like Nero, fiddling while our Rome burned!" Henry tried hard to think how such a conflagration could have started. Had he left a lamp alight somewhere in the mill? Had someone committed arson for some reason? Had he any enemies who could have done such a thing? All these thoughts charged his mind as they drew nearer and nearer to the scene. Mrs Gritton dissolved in sobs and tears and others around her sought to comfort her. As they drew nearer they could see that the mill cottage was not affected, though the heat must have been enormous. The wind which was so often enjoyed as making work possible now played its part in destroying to the last embers the great mill with all its workings, mills stones and cog wheels.

It was the Rector who drove his trap near to Henry's wagon and said, "Henry, God came to Moses in the burning bush, let God come to you in this hour of fiery destruction. Don't let your trust be lost when it is most on trial. I will stand with you and the day will come when we shall stand together at the mill stones and sing in victory as we have done this night in the Cathedral!"

It was two full years before the mill was rebuilt and restored to full working order. It would have been much longer but for the fact that out on Bodmin Moor a derelict mill was up for sale just when Henry was needing some parts to replace those burned in the fire. The Rector and a number of the parish council made their way up to the mill on this particular morning and stood together around the mill stones as they turned for the first time and all sang as they had so joyously done in Truro Cathedral on the night of the tragedy. This time instead of Handel's great oratorio, they all sang one of Charles Wesley's new hymns, so beloved of Henry and his Methodist society. Mrs Gritton called them all to enjoy a newly baked scone and at the forefront of the company was Captain Williams with his large handkerchief spread across his chest in readiness.

During the long days awaiting the rebuilding of the mill, Henry Gritton and his wife had spent many hours in the evenings with the Rector and Alicia around the rectory fireside. It became a second home to them and following the restarting of the mill such an arrangement was continued as the Rector's children, there were two now that Elizabeth May had joined John Henry, were treated as their adopted grandchildren. The Gritton's had never been blessed with children and so Alicia was to them the daughter they had never had.

It was during one of these evenings whilst they were deep in discussion that a loud knock came at the door of the rectory.

"Who can be calling at this late hour?" said the Rector calling to Mrs Jones that he would answer the door himself. On opening it he was faced with a bearded man dressed very much as the Rector dressed, obviously a fellow priest.

"Come in good Sir, what brings you to Lower Penzle at such an hour?"

Removing his hat the man stepped into the hallway and was relieved of his coat and shown into the study, where John and his company were sitting. He excused himself apologising for disturbing them and was asked to please be seated.

"You may well wonder why I am here and when I tell you, you may be somewhat shocked, though I trust not disturbed as when I last called upon you."

"You have called on us before? Pray tell us when, for I have no recollection of such a visit."

"Rector it was in this very room that we last met some four years since."

"Whilst your voice is somewhat familiar I cannot recall

the occasion, please tell us more."

The stranger continued as they all viewed him with questionable doubts. "On that occasion, Sir, I held you at knife point and robbed you of your horse."

"Oh, now I think I understand, Sir. You are the man we chased across the English Channel. You are the escaped convict," remembered the Rector.

"Yes, indeed I am the same. I am even this night in disguise as a man of the cloth for good reason. I am still on the run, though returning to my home county in the hope of clearing my name. The foul crime of which I was accused has, I believe been resurrected because another man has boasted that he performed it as he is now in Launceston himself."

"And how do you know all this?" asked the Rector, all the room agog with interest.

"You may recall that I landed that old tub the *Sea Winkle* on Jersey Island and there the soldiers hunted for a while, but I eluded them until they gave up the chase and I settled with a farmer and have lived there ever since that day."

"Do I understand that you have heard your news and have returned to clear your name here in Cornwall?"

"That is correct and with your help I may be able to do that, but I fear you may feel unable or unwilling to help me after my behaviour that last time I was in this room. Please forgive my hiding under this present false identity, good Sir, but I found it much easier to sail in the *Sea Winkle* thus adorned, though the good Captain Storeton had never seen my face before as you have."

The Rector called Mrs Jones into the room, introduced the visitor, and as she let out a little gasp, was assured that there was now no danger, for her or the children up stairs asleep in their beds.

"Mrs Jones, will you get a bed ready for our friend, he will be staying tonight and indeed several nights I think."

"You are so kind, Sir. I heard tales of you and your adventures while on the island. That is why I was bold enough to come to your door tonight."

At this point Henry Gritton and his wife bade them all 'Good Night' and climbing into their trap, they left the Rector's household to look after this strange caller, requesting that they be kept informed as to how his case might unfold.

The following morning over breakfast more of the man's story was revealed. He had at one time attempted a course of training at Trevecca College under John Fletcher.

"Sir," said Alicia amazed at this news, "John Fletcher officiated at our marriage, maybe he will stand a reference for you if there is a court case!"

"That I am sure he would, if only we can get the case reopened safely. My fear is that if what I have heard proved false, I would again be under arrest and bound for deportation as before. And this time I would be treated as an escaped man and treated more severely than before."

"I think we should wait until I can get contact with the Magistrate in Truro. We know him well and he does not need at this time to know you are here. I will leave you at Henry Gritton's mill this morning, there you will cause fewer questions than here at the rectory and I will ride over to Truro and see how the land lies with the magistrate." As decisive as ever the Rector had his plans.

The Rector of Lower Penzle

Chapter Twelve

The Ring of Truth

Henry Gritton was delighted to receive Jonathan Squires into the mill and give him work to do, stating that he was simply an employee for the season and welcome help as the renewed mill got back into full swing. The wind was as fresh as ever on the hill top and farmers were only too glad to have a mill in their locality again. Jonathan Squires had been working manually in Jersey for these last four years and was well able and willing to do all that was asked of him, but more than his work, his background intrigued Henry Gritton. As an ardent Methodist, Henry was well acquainted with the history of Trevecca and so the two men had much to discuss. The mention of John Fletcher in that first conversation in the rectory caused Henry to query whether John Fletcher would now be in any way able to help as he was no longer at Trevecca. Henry informed Jonathan of the differences between John Fletcher and Lady Huntington and their parting, Lady Huntington being the patron of Trevecca. But deeper in their conversations Henry was wanting to know what caused Jonathan to give up his attempts at training for the priesthood.

Evening by evening after a heavy working day the two men talked into the early hours of the next day. This was food and drink to Henry and his Methodist fervour.

"My father is a high churchman," said Jonathan, "He also was an admirer of John Wesley."

However, when Wesley preached against the Calvinistic cause, Jonathan's father parted company, so when Jonathan announced that he was to train with the godly vicar of Madeley, John Fletcher! he was told not to expect any support from his father. Jonathan was more or less cut off from home and money. For a while he managed to scrape along, but eventually he gave up and returned to ordinary work. It was during this time that he found himself in very bad company and when a murder was committed in the tavern where he was lodging, he was accused and convicted and so became a member of the convict community.

All this Henry Gritton understood better than most as he was well read in theology and the doctrines Wesley stood for. Together the men not only talked, but prayed and on the occasions that the Rector visited they joined together in that act. Finally, the Rector was able to bring some news of a possible resurrection of the case and an appeal for a retrial. In this instant there was no possibility of the Rector taking a legal position as he had in his own defence in smuggling days. The case was prepared and witnesses found and a date set.

Together, the Rector, Henry Gritton, Alicia and Jonathan rode over to Truro to prepare for the trial. A barrister was appointed and agreed to defend the case.

The prisoner in Launceston Gail was carefully

questioned as to his supposed confession and as they expected denied any such confession. But then one of the other prisoners was also interrogated and gave a clear statement of such a confession being made to him a year before as the guilty man boasted of all he had got away with during a life of crime. The prisoner requested anonymity and hoped he would not be needed in giving witness to his statement. Much discussion was held with the barrister and the local magistrate and it seemed that this could be granted if the defending lawyer was willing to accept the witness statement.

Little by little the case was prepared and eventually the day arrived when the court opened the case to retry Jonathan Squires. A military presence was in court to verify that the accused was an escaped convict previously found guilty, tried and sentenced. Jonathan, while confident of his innocence was also aware that the case had previously been strongly against him circumstantially, he being the only man in the tavern that night in the room with the murdered man. The facts were laid out by the Crown at great length from the records of the first trial and as the Crown's barrister concluded his case it seemed that a jury would again vote in favour of a guilty verdict.

Then the barrister for the defence stood and agreed that his client was indeed in the murdered man's room that night, but argued that he was sound asleep and knew nothing of the crime until he was awakened by the innkeeper and accused of the crime. Certain property of the dead man was scattered about the room and yet none was ever found in the possession of the accused. There was however a large ring of the dead man which was missing and this had been found in the possession of the confessed murderer here in the prison. He had claimed it as his own but the innkeeper had witnessed the murdered man wearing the ring on the night he was murdered. This fact had not come to the attention of anyone at the original trial, but now caused a great stir among the jury and visitors in the court. The confessed murderer was brought into the dock and there challenged regarding the ring. He vehemently claimed it as his own. The innkeeper was again questioned and testified clearly that he had seen the murdered man wearing the ring that very night. The defending barrister closed his case and the jury gathered to state their verdict on the originally accused. NOT GUILTY!

Relieved, Jonathan Squires called out "Praise God, I'm free!" And the judge called for the now guilty man to be charged and tried at a future date, returning him to Launceston Jail forthwith. Together the little party from Lower Penzle made their way to the local tavern for a hearty meal and then rode home in Henry Gritton's cart.

"Well, Jonathan, what next? Will you be thinking of returning to the possibility of entering the priesthood?" Jonathan and the Rector spent a day or so in such talk.

"Well, Sir, I ought to look for my father and mother who have not seen me in these four years and probably think I'm either dead or in some far away colony. But my real intention is to contact Mr Fletcher at Madeley. I think he can guide me best for the future. Having had this period of trial, I feel ready to get down to some serious study and a vocation. There must be many out there in the parishes that need the encouragement I have received. If I am thought worthy, I would gladly devote my life to God's service," was Jonathan's reply.

"Jonathan, none of us are worthy of such service, but by the grace of God, we can accept such a calling in humility.

I think you would find a welcome by John Fletcher and no one could help you more than that saintly man of God."

And with this exchange, Jonathan Squires once again took his leave of the Rector and his family. But just as he was leaving, he asked the Rector to solve a problem that had plagued him ever since he left on horseback for what turned out to be a chase across the English Channel.

"Sir, when I had the impudence to lock you and your family in your study, I saddled your horse and then came back to release you from the study. When I entered the room you had all disappeared and I have never known how you could have done so?"

"Jonathan that is a little secret you must never know, so let us leave with your question and your problem unanswered! Farewell my friend, and may the Lord be with you as you find your parents and seek dear John Fletcher."

Jonathan left the rectory and walked down to catch the coach which would take him on to Crendon Bywater and London, a free man.

On the quayside at Crendon Bywater, Jonathan found the captain of the *Sea Winkle* quietly sitting alongside his worthy old vessel.

"Can I help you Sir?" he asked the stranger. "Why, it's the gentleman I shipped from the Channel Isles but a few weeks ago."

"That's right," said Jonathan, "But you need to hear my story, for you knew not just who you were carrying across the Channel at that time."

Sitting alongside the captain, Jonathan Squires told his story and apologised for stealing the captain's vessel four years previously. Captain Storeton looked long and hard at the now clean shaven man beside him and found it hard to see the same man.

"I suppose I should have you arrested this very moment for stealing my ship, but seeing you have gone through such an ordeal, I'm happy enough to wish you well and the Rector and I will have a good laugh when we next meet."

Chapter Thirteen

A Mine of Information

The Rector sat enjoying an evening meal with Jeremiah Solent the innkeeper. Alicia, the Rector's wife, had gone over to the North coast with their two children to visit relatives as Mrs Jones, the Rector's housekeeper, and Mrs Solent, the innkeeper's wife, had gone to South Wales to visit their relatives, following a busy Easter both at the inn and the church. Mrs Jones had married a native of Aberbeeg in the Ebbw Valley and so she was always welcomed home by her in-laws, the Jones' of Abercommin Farm above the little village of Aberbeeg. She was especially looking forward to this visit as she had been informed that the Rev John Wesley was to preach in the Aberbeeg Parish church at the very top of the hill. The vicar was not an admirer of Wesley; he was far too much of an enthusiast for his liking. But it was a certainty that such a visitor would draw a huge crowd to this rather isolated spot for once and that could harvest a good collection during the service. He only hoped that it would not lead to a riot, for even that was not unusual when

Wesley was about. Mrs Jones had never forgotten her first experience of Wesley at Gwennap Pit as she with so many from around the Cornish countryside had gathered to hear the famous man.

Now bereft of his family and housekeeper, the Rector was glad to share a meal around the fireside of the White Horses. As the little company sat and enjoyed the closing moments of the day, a late visitor entered from the parlour of the White Horses and asked for the innkeeper.

"I'm here, Molly," he called to his housemaid who was attending to the bar.

With that the visitor entered the rear parlour and introduced himself.

"Good landlord, I need a room for the night or maybe several nights. Can you offer such?"

"Why yes, and you are welcome to Lower Penzle, Sir."

"I'm Peter Tring of London, Sir and I'll likely be staying for a day or so."

"Well, come you in Sir and I've no doubt you will be needing a meal if you've come a journey."

"That is indeed true, good landlord, I've recently arrived on the Plymouth coach and had difficulty finding accommodation in Crendon Bywater, so got a lift with a carter down into the village. The man was as deaf as a post, so all the countryside will know by now that I'm here, for I had to shout enough to wake the dead in every grave yard for miles."

"Oh, that'll be Ben Pearson, and you're right about letting everyone know, for we all let him do the talking when we get a lift on his old cart. Well let me take your coat, Sir. This is Rector Trevethin, come and share our fireside while I get you some food."

"And what brings you to our neck of the woods, Sir?"

asked the Rector in a casual manner which did not seem to be offensive to the visitor.

"Oh, I happen to have received a small piece of land as part of an inheritance from a distant relative. It's been some time since, but only now have I found time to follow it up, though it may still prove to be a waste of time and energy."

"And is this land in our parish?"

"I'm not sure but on the map it was shown as being below Conbury Beacon a few hundred yards from the shore."

"Oh, then it is indeed within our parish for I ride out there often when taking the air. Would it have a small building on the site?"

"Why yes, I understand that originally it was the head of a mine shaft, but that was never developed," replied the visitor with a seeming willingness to follow the information.

"Now sit ye down Sir, and enjoy some cold mutton and potatoes and the maid will bring you a tankard of ale. There's newly baked bread, too, so enjoy it, though I do apologise that there is nothing hot at this time of the night and with my wife away and us not expecting customers at this hour."

Jeremiah settled himself beside the Rector and joined in the conversation. "Did I hear you mention Conbury Beacon, Sir? Then you must be referring to Treowen's Folly. It's not much of a building and I guess it's more a hideout for foxes and sheep these days. No one's bothered with it since I've been landlord of the White Horses and I guess a few years before that, too."

"Well," continued the visitor, glad of such information as was gathered in such company, "beneath that building I understand there is or at least, was, a mine shaft driven vertically down into the cliff top."

"Aye, you're right there, but I shouldn't wonder that it's long since caved in and won't have much to show for itself these days."

"You're right there," added the Rector, "for when Alicia and I were out riding in our courting days we sought shelter there and found it full of sheep dirt and I shouldn't wonder that there's not a dead ewe or lamb in there by the smell. Let me offer to ride out with you tomorrow, Sir, you may have my wife's horse, if you ride and I'll be glad to show you the delights of my hill-top ride."

And with that promise, the little company rose, the Rector for his own home and the visitor to the comfort offered by the White Horses.

The following morning Peter Tring walked up to the rectory and together with the Rector rode out on the blustery cliff top to Treowen's Folly on Conbury Beacon. The Rector had been right in his suspicions about some dead animal in the ruin. It was a foul stench that met the two men as they looked inside the tumbled down walls of what remained of a building. But with no roof over head the light showed plainly that what had been a shaft was still evident, now but a deep cavity in the earthy floor covered in a mire of sheep droppings.

"Well, there's not much to show for my inheritance, Rector, but I will seek some labour and clean out the muck and see just how deep the original shaft went."

And with that the two men rode back to the village and a meal with the landlord of the White Horses.

Any visitor staying in the village for a few days caused tongues to wag and it was not long before Captain Winton Willoughby Williams paid a rare visit to the White Horses to survey the new arrival and seek an introduction. His excuse was to announce himself as sexton of the church with an invitation to Sunday services. The visitor was impressed with his keenness and accepted a seat beside the Captain and Mrs Williams with a further invitation to Sunday lunch which was all that could be desired under former widow Adams, now Mrs Williams', cooking.

The conversation soon turned to the subject of Peter Tring's ownership of Treowen's Folly and his desire for labourers to do some clearing of the inside of such walls as were standing. Captain Williams readily put himself forward as foreman of the works, and Peter, not wishing to offend his host accepted, believing Captain Williams would recruit such help to carry out the job. Within the next week, not only was the dirt cleared from the building, but clear evidence shown of a fairly deep shaft now somewhat filled in, but still there to be revealed by some extra digging. Ropes were tethered to the beams of what had been a roof and men were lowered into the shaft as it was excavated further day by day. Lanterns were lowered into the darkened shaft until it was felt too dangerous to dig without shoring up the sides. Then, as Peter himself descended, he looked around the walls of the shaft to catch any signs of metal ore glinting in this old mine.

Cornwall was renowned for tin and copper and Peter had some expectations as he surveyed the walls of the shaft. Then, as he had himself lowered to the bottom of the shaft, his feet felt something soft. He shone his lantern below him on the ground. At first he thought he must be treading on a dead sheep's carcass, but as he looked more closely, he realised it was the decomposed body of a man. Horrified, he called to be hoisted up and shocked he told the men of his find and said there would be no more digging that day. Peter made his way back to the village, calling on the Rector as he did, telling him of his find.

The Rector called on the chairman of his parish council, Joseph Trenbeath and listened as Joseph told of a man who had disappeared many years before and no one had ever found trace of him. Together the parish councillors made a team to exhume the body and try to find some identifying marks on what was left of his clothing. Joseph inspected the parish register for funerals and found a name with a note stating that a funeral was held without a body. This was some fifty years before Joseph was chairman, indeed he was but a young lad. Now they were all to wonder if this was the solution to an age old mystery which had long been forgotten.

Peter stopped all digging and after a burial had taken place went back to his home in London to search again the papers of his distant relative. Eventually he came across a diary and in it an account of the sinking of the mine shaft and the hopes of great wealth from the tin mining industry in this Cornish acquisition. It was obvious that digging had been much more extensive than Peter's attempts had uncovered. Then on a day when his relative had pressed his workers hard for results and news had come up the shaft that they had found a great seam a man had fallen to his death down the shaft. All had fled from the workings and the site was vacated, never to be worked again. Peter read each word in the diary and realised what effect such a tragedy had had on his relative and vowed to have the shaft filled in and he personally would pay for a head stone in the lost man's memory to be placed in the Lower Penzle church yard.

As Peter read all the detail of what had happened he saw plainly that greed had driven his relative to seek wealth only to take a man's life. Had his relative ever sought the family of the dead man? Had they ever known what had happened? The truth had never been revealed by those who knew it and someone had just been left as though lost at sea or on a journey. Maybe those who knew had been paid to keep quiet, or was there a more sinister truth that the man didn't just fall, but was pushed to his death and all were sworn to silence? Peter Tring came back to Lower Penzle simply to see the headstone placed on the grave, but then went back to London and Lower Penzle buried again the mystery of Treowen's Folly.

The cliff-top rides were never quite as attractive again. Just to pass the Folly was to recall the tragedy and wish answers could be given to those who long before had lost a husband, father or son. The Rector could only guess that he must have come from some distant parish or maybe from the Channel Isles or Ireland. There would never be an answer as to who he was or why the silence at his death.

The Rector of Lower Penzle

Chapter Fourteen

"...And the Greatest of These is Love"

"Twenty five years is a long time, Rector, much has happened and surely everyone will be wanting to celebrate such a time."

The speaker was Donald Creedy the recently elected chairman of the parish council. And he was remonstrating with the Rector for the reluctance he was showing to any celebration of his Silver Wedding Anniversary.

"I suppose you are right, Donald, but I know Alicia would not want a great fuss any more than I do. We would value a brief service, but other than that, what are you thinking of?"

The Rector saw the keenness of Donald and knew it was a reflection of the whole council and maybe the whole community, so he accepted that he must acquiesce.

And so it transpired that on the anniversary day the whole parish gathered in the church, even though a few were anything but regular members of the Rector's congregation. Added to the communicants of St Matthew's were Henry and Mrs Gritton, fervent Methodists, and many from the outlying farms outside the parish boundaries of Lower Penzle. He could imagine that there was a time when the Rector's bachelordom was the talking point of every eligible young lady and few could easily recall just how Alicia Mary Gritton had come into contact with her future husband. But one thing was sure, this was a marriage made in heaven, for with a fine son, John Henry, and daughter, Elizabeth May, they made as happy a family as any in the parish or county.

The service of thanksgiving was conducted by the Bishop of Truro and a speech was made by Captain Winton Willoughby Williams with great gusto and flourish so that when all sat down to enjoy the meal supplied by a now elderly Jeremiah Solent of the White Horses Inn, there was a mood of great affection for the Rector and his wife. It was the Rector who decided to add to the occasion a few words of thanksgiving, both to the God who he suggested brought about this change in his affairs, and the villagers of Lower Penzle who had shared in so many of the exciting events of John's ministry. He recounted the days of smuggling when Captain Williams was so often deceived, of the days when men and women from the Bastille were brought out of France and rescued from the guillotine. He recounted the tragic fall of Alicia and her temporary blindness, of the birth of his son and daughter as gifts from a loving God far more than he could ever have deserved. John Trevethin concluded his brief speech with thanks to his parish council for their loyalty over these past years and adventures and even Captain Williams for not being smart enough to catch him sooner, to which there was a great guffaw and a very red faced Captain to acknowledge that he had at last managed to catch the rascal red handed! And so the day ended with the whole company joining with the Rector in reciting *The Lord's Prayer*.

It was this note that caused a voice to follow the "amen," with a strong French accent and all hushed to listen to the stranger, an old man who had quietly joined with them without anyone realising he was a stranger.

"Friend," called the Rector, "how come you are with us today?"

"Rector, you will recall a certain voyage home from France on the good ship *Sea Winkle*, will you not? You read this very prayer to me as with tears I acknowledged your kindness to me in rescuing me from the very system I had helped to create but which had turned its wrath on its own subjects."

"Why, I do believe it is Pierre Latreque!" The whole company was transfixed as the two men faced each other and then rushed to embrace. "Pierre, I would hardly have known you were here, how wonderful that you should join us for this day of thanksgiving." The Rector was almost in tears.

"My dear Rector, I was present at your marriage, it is only fitting that I should be here today, for I too, have much to be thankful for both to you and to the God whom you serve and gave you such a spirit of forgiveness that you could put your life in jeopardy to save your enemy. Thank you a thousand times dear friend."

As the whole company dispersed from the lawns of the rectory, four people rode out of the village to Crendon Bywater where a very old *Sea Winkle* was awaiting to carry them out to the Isles of Scilly. Call it a second honeymoon if you like but for John and Alicia it was an opportunity to introduce John Henry and Elizabeth May to the delights of a sea washed beauty spot which had first sealed their parent's marriage and their future together. They called it "Smuggler's Love."

Chapter Fifteen

A Storm in the Bishop's Teacup

The Reverend John Trevethin was a loyal churchman of the Anglican Communion. He was not among those who had separated from the church following the great 1662 division which had carried so many out of their pulpit and formed the non-conformist groups all over the country. But having said that, he was deeply interested in the evangelical movement of John Wesley and his followers amongst whom he cherished the friendship of Henry Gritton the miller of Lower Penzle. Henry was not only a fine man at his job, milling the grain from far and wide, but he was a deeply committed follower of John Wesley, leading a strong group of those who had several years before the Rector's coming to St Matthews, separated themselves into a Methodist society. John had spent many hours with Henry, both out of an interest in their theological thinking and of course since John had married Henry's niece.

The Rector was a fine musician, playing the violin that

held a critical eye on the music of his church, challenging the choir to accept many of the new hymns coming from the pen of Charles Wesley, brother and John's companion in the Methodist movement.

Indeed, it was this interest that brought John into somewhat of a conflict with his Bishop and found him on this day, awaiting an interview outside the Bishop's study in Truro's Cathedral Square. News had been carried to the Bishop of John Trevethin's Methodist interests and the Bishop was determined that any division should not be brought about in his diocese.

This was no light dismissal of Methodism, for the Bishop was a man much exercised by the writings of John Newton and William Cowper, known in church circles as the Olney Group, much opposed to the Wesley's. So John Trevethin sat somewhat uneasily awaiting the interview. Henry Gritton had travelled with John to Truro, but had not accompanied him into the Bishop's abode. He had agreed to await the outcome of the interview and pray that all would go well for his friend.

The study door opened and John was called into the room by the Bishop's servant. It was a room lined with books and the Bishop sat behind a large mahogany desk. He rose to greet the Rector and bade him be seated.

"John, you know my reason for calling you to this conversation."

"Yes, I read your note carefully."

"Well," continued the Bishop, "I am deeply concerned that your interest in these matters will bring about a division within my diocese and I am not going to allow such to take place at any cost."

"Bishop, I fully understand your concern, but feel it is quite groundless, as I would be the last to countenance

124

such in my parish. But I have to admit that the teaching of the Wesley's has a great deal to commend it and my parish councilors have spent many hours discussing these matters, feeling that we must seriously consider where we stand."

"Quite, quite, I appreciate that you are a thoughtful parish priest, John and have quite a reputation both in matters of faith and matters that are not quite the usual. But at the moment, I am concerned that Sir Richard Crendon has once again felt led to complain of your pulpit pronouncements, not this time about his activities, but about your interference with his own parish priest's preaching."

"Sir," replied the Rector, "I admit a difference in our theological position, but at no time have I transgressed into Crendon Bywater territory or held meetings in that parish. The fact that my Methodist friends have held such meetings is entirely their responsibility. The fact that I attended such was as a lay-person and not in my capacity as a priest."

"Well, be that as it may, it was at best a lack of tact on your part and I fully agree with Sir Richard that you ought not to do so in the future."

"I am willing to accept your admonition, Bishop, but I must add that if I am able to have John or Charles Wesley in my pulpit I will welcome them, but to be absolutely fair I would as easily welcome any of the Olney Group, too. You see Bishop, whilst I love the Anglican Communion and honour my loyalty to you as my Bishop, I have a greater love and that is to the Lord whom we serve and a loyalty to the truth we are called to preach."

John stood looking the Bishop full in the eye.

"John, I have no doubt of your loyalty, but knowing you I suppose I must accept that you are no ordinary man of the cloth. I think I must accept yours is a smuggler's love, whatever that might mean."

The interview was over and in a tea shop just a few yards from the cathedral, John Trevethin and Henry Gritton met to once again confirm a friendship which had led to the smuggler's love of Henry's niece and the Rector's break with bachelordom to a life of married bliss!

"I'm afraid this was just a storm in a tea cup, Henry, and whilst I pay no attention to reading tea leaves, I somehow think the storm once again brings us into conflict with our friend at Crendon Hall. And by that I am little disturbed. There are greater storms we have faced in days long past. But, Henry, the Bishop said something which took me back to our past and I wonder just what it means myself?"

"And what did the Bishop say, John?"

"Well, he said mine was a smuggler's love! What would you say he meant by that?"

"Oh, there's no doubt in my mind that you will forever find yourself known by your past escapades in these parts and who knows what pictures will be painted by those who knew you in another guise. You cannot expect the events of such to be forgotten, at least not while you have Captain Winton Willoughby Williams in your congregation."